Return of the Gunfighter

While eking out a precarious livelihood rearing pigs, ex bank robber Randy Cole has been asked to help a homesteader who is being threatened with eviction. The ageing gunfighter is loath once again to take up arms until he learns that the victim is an old side-kick. And the skunk entrusted with the eviction is Jute Farley who betrayed the Cole gang and was responsible for Randy spending the next ten years in jail.

Now Randy must exact his own lethal brand of justice. But the trail is littered with deadly varmints and much blood will be shed before the final showdown.

By the same author

Dead Man Walking
Two for Texas
Divided Loyalties

Writing as Dale Graham

High Plains Vendetta
Dance with the Devil
Nugget!
Montezuma's Legacy
Death Rides Alone
Gambler's Dawn
Vengeance at Bittersweet
Justice for Crockett
Bluecoat Renegade

Return of the Gunfighter

Ethan Flagg

ROBERT HALE · LONDON

First published in Great Britain 2009

ISBN 978-0-7090-8751-9

Robert Hale Limited
Clerkenwell House
Clerkenwell Green
London EC1R 0HT

www.halebooks.com

Typeset by
Derek Doyle & Associates, Shaw Heath
Printed and bound in Great Britain by
CPI Antony Rowe, Chippenham and Eastbourne

ONE

NO GOING BACK

Clint Bowdry was seated on the veranda outside his Utah farmhouse. It was a fine spring morning. The early mist had lifted to reveal clusters of small flowers assiduously cultivated by Jan, his adored wife of twelve years. The differing shades added a welcome touch of colour to the dun landscape stretching away towards the distant upsurge of the Henry Mountains.

Gently nudging the old rocking chair into motion, he puffed on his clay pipe. It ought to have been the action of a guy at peace with the world, but Clint Bowdry was a troubled man. His disquiet showed itself in the taut lines of a weathered face and the deep furrows creasing his forehead.

A dozen sheep had been butchered the previous day. It was the third such incident in as many weeks. And he had a good idea who was behind the brutal deeds. Clint's face hardened as he recalled the threats made to him and his family if they didn't pay their arrears to the newly established Green River Development Agency.

Of course, there was no actual proof that the company was behind the intimidatory tactics. Those skunks were too clever for that. When challenged, the manager, Jethro Tindale, had denied all knowledge of any such skulduggery. Indeed he had taken umbrage at the very idea that he could resort to such heinous actions. His play-acting might have been convincing to a less sardonic individual.

But Clint Bowdry was not to be hoodwinked.

This sort of thing would never have happened under the previous manager, he surmised, blowing out a spume of blue smoke. Hiram Tasker had been a fair-minded land agent. But he had retired and the company had been taken over by a business consortium based in the state capital of Salt Lake City.

Clint scowled as Tindale's unctuous smiles impinged themselves on his brain. He puffed hard on the pipe gripping the thin stem with his teeth. Sewer rats like that always got others to do their dirty work; gunmen like Jute Farley and his gang of mean-eyed hardcases.

Five days previously, the whole gang had arrived unannounced, and bristling with openly displayed weaponry. They had deliberately trampled across the maize crop adjoining the farm access track.

Reining up in front of the farmhouse, Farley had thrown down an envelope.

'You've got a week to comply with this writ,' he

growled, 'otherwise me and the boys will have to . . .' He paused to emphasize his next comment aiming a leery grin at his henchmen before continuing, 'help you come up with the right decision.'

There were ribald guffaws all round from the menacing body.

'And just to let you know we mean business,' added Farley, drawing his pistol, 'here's some of what you can expect.'

He pointed the Smith & Wesson .44 at a cluster of squawking Leghorns and let rip. A flutter of white feathers lifted skyward stained a deep red with chicken blood. Six live birds were now reduced to three.

Clint grabbed for his own revolver.

'You no good sidewinder,' he blazed unwittingly as a red mist clouded his normally astute judgement.

It was Jan who saved him from an early grave. Settling a slim yet firm hand over his own, she urged caution while holding the gunman's simpering gaze with a fixed regard.

'Easy there, Clint,' she soothed in a level yet staunch tone. 'No sense in getting yourself killed over a few chickens.'

Clint's body was tight as a drumhead. His entire being itched to throw down on this festering toad. Only his wife's cogent advice stayed his hand. Slowly the haze lifted as clarity and a sane assessment of the ominous situation reasserted itself in his fevered brain.

'You have a wise woman there, Bowdry,' smirked

the gang leader, once he realized the danger was past. Openly, he cast a salacious eye over the comely female form. 'Best to heed her advice.' With that final remark, he wheeled about and headed off back towards Monticello, followed by his sidekicks. They were left with a parting threat that drifted menacingly in the tense atmosphere. 'One week, remember, then watch yer back!'

And that week was almost up.

For the umpteenth time Clint studied the official-looking writ, scowling at the final words stating that should he be unable to repay his debt, *proceedings would be taken according to the rule of law.*

Clint scoffed. He screwed the document into a ball and flung it away.

The only rule of law likely to be enforced here would be *gun law* under the auspices of Jute Farley.

But he was ready for anything that the gang could throw at him. Or so he hoped.

All Clint Bowdry needed was another couple of months until the spring lambs could be sold, then he would have paid off his debts in full. Was that asking too much? it wasn't his fault that successive droughts had decimated the maize yield. Tindale appeared to be deliberately targeting landowners ekeing out a living in the Dirty Devil Valley. Already, two of Clint's neighbours had sold up, forced out by threats and intimidation.

But the dirt farmer reckoned himself to be made of sterner stuff. No way was he going to be pushed off his land without a fight. Indeed, he was determined they would have to carry him out in a pine box first.

His hand reached down to the Loomis shotgun, now always within easy reach.

'You sure we're doing the right thing, Clint?'

Jan Bowdry handed her husband a mug of coffee. Her words contained a measure of worried concern. She knew exactly what Clint was thinking. A pragmatic woman, her main concern was for the safety of her family, especially that of her young son. The three of them standing up to the ruthless determination of six hardened gun hands was not to be considered lightly.

But Clint had an obstinate streak. And he doggedly refused to be browbeaten by any jumped-up company man trying to bulldog him.

'Durned right we are, gal,' he averred with unequivocal conviction. 'No goddamned office crank is gonna cheat me out of my rights.' His tight jaw intimated that there was no room for negotiation. Right was on his side and he was not about to toss it aside.

Jan sighed, then shrugged resignedly and went back into the house to prepare breakfast. A dark frown clouded her otherwise smooth countenance.

Although of similar age to her husband, Jan Bowdry carried her years well. Clint, on the other hand, possessed a gnarled appearance such that he could easily be mistaken for her father.

The streaks of silver that had invaded Jan's thick wavy hair merely added to her charisma. In contrast to many wives who had succumbed to the arduous toil of life on the frontier, Jan Bowdry had always taken a pride in her appearance. It showed in the uprightly handsome bearing, an obvious fact that Clint had never once taken for granted.

For her part, Jan was forever grateful that he had accepted her condition without question when they had first started walking out together. Never once had the source ot her carrying young Luke been held against her. The boy's natural father had remained locked inside her heart. If Clint had ever deigned to enquire, she would have revealed all. But he never had.

Marriage had followed as easily as day follows night. Bringing up another man's offspring was something that only the most special of men would accept. And she loved Clint all the more for his commitment to Luke.

But now, all their hopes and dreams seemed to have been put in jeopardy.

On numerous occasions Jan had witnessed her husband's stubborn obsession when it came to redressing a misdeed.

The most recent had occurred only the previous month when a travelling drummer had called by selling a new strain of quick-ripening maize seed. Clint had been impressed by the dude's blarney and had bought enough for the whole of the acreage under the plough. After learning from a friend that the claim was worthless and the seed contaminated, Clint had displayed no hesitation in pursuing the miscreant and exacting full and conclusive retribution.

It took him a week to locate the culprit.

Upon his return, all he would say was that the guy would not be deceiving other farmers for a long time to come. Jan considered it prudent not enquire any further into the fate of the unfortunate fraudster.

At that moment, her worried thoughts were interrupted by an urgent summons from outside.

'Riders coming in.'

She hurried back outside. Clint was on his feet, the Loomis gripped tightly revealing blanched knuckles.

A swirling cloud of yellow dust concealed the approaching visitors. Soon the blurred outline of a wagon drawn by a team of four hove into view. Both of the watchers relaxed.

It was only Bill Flaxman. As he drew closer, it was clear that his neighbour was not here on a social call.

Flaxman reined up outside the house. Clint eyed the wagon piled high with the family's personal effects. It was obvious they were pulling out.

'You leaving then, Bill'?'

The question didn't need asking. But Flaxman nevertheless supplied the answer.

'Me and Belle felt it better to accept Tindale's offer before any more accidents happen,' he said in a morose tone.

'What they done this time?' rasped Clint.

'Burnt out the east cornfield and killed the cow,' replied the disconsolate farmer.

'We have our children to consider,' added his wife in support, jabbing a thumb at two youngsters huddled in the back amidst the clutter.

'What you gonna do then, Clint?' asked Flaxman. 'Wait for 'em to burn you out? Do that and you'll have nothin' to sell. I'd accept Tindale's offer and clear out while you got the chance.' His next remark was aimed at Jan. 'Cain't you persuade this stubborn old cuss to see sense, Mrs Bowdry?'

Jan drew herself up and took hold of her husband's hand.

'If Clint chooses to stay then I'm with him all the way.' The flinty gleam in her brown eyes burned bright and unapologetic. Luke had joined his parents. In his hands he held a Sharps hunting rifle, an ancient .36 Navy Colt slotted into the leather belt holding up his frayed trousers. He was a boy fast becoming a man. And it was obvious to all where his loyalties lay.

'Then on your heads be it,' muttered Flaxman.

There was a macabre sense of finality in his words. Whipping up the team, the small party moved out. No further words were passed as they disappeared from sight.

So the die had been cast. There was no going back now.

Jan felt a cold shiver ripple through her slim frame.

TWO

PAINFUL RECALL

'Why do you have to be such a cantankerous swine?'

The mumbled complaint was not issued in a particularly virulent manner even though the pig farmer was splattered with mud. Manhandling a large and heavily pregnant sow into more congenial surroundings in readiness for farrowing took a heap of care and persuasion. Thus far the obstinate old gal had resisted all his efforts.

But Randy Cole was no stranger to dealing with recalcitrant individuals, be it human or animal, and he knew that his way would prevail in the end. None the less, he would have preferred it to be sooner rather than later.

Edging the sow once more in the direction of the farrowing shed, his attention was distracted by the glint of sunlight on metal. A curious eye strayed to the far side of the enclosure. As Randy straightened his back to investigate the strange phenomenon, the sow took the opportunity to scuttle out of reach.

Randy screwed up his eyes to filter out the strong rays of a lowering afternoon sun.

A boy of around twelve years stared back at him. The kid was stick thin but carried himself with an easy grace atop the fine black stallion. And there was no mistaking the confident manner in which he held the Sharps rifle. Lank hair the colour of ripe corn poked from beneath a slouch hat that had long since abandoned its original shape.

It concealed most of the kid's face but there was no disguising the look of contempt offered by the sullen mouth. The obvious derision at what he was witnessing was bolstered by an insolent snort.

The farmer stiffened.

'You want something, boy?' he enquired tersely. He had come across such reactions to his choice of work previously. But from one so young, the arrogant sneer stuck in his craw. As a kid, he had always been brought up to respect his elders.

'Don't reckon I do . . . now,' came back the equally curt rejoinder.

'And what's that supposed to mean?' rapped Cole, his leathery features colouring as the sap rose. Where humans were concerned, he was not the most patient of jiggers.

'I came looking for a tough, hard-ass gunfighter.' The kid almost spat the words out. 'But all I found was some sad excuse of a man covered in pig dung. Reckon I'll just have to look elsewhere for help.'

The cussed insult was the final straw. Randy emitted a raucous bellow of rage and made to rectify the slur in time-honoured fashion using the flat of his belt. But he hadn't counted on the cloying nature of the mud. As a result he tumbled ungainly into the foul-smelling ooze.

The kid hooted with laughter. But it was short-lived. A doleful expression clouded his youthful features. It was matched by an equally melancholic inference.

'Don't know what my pa must have been thinking when he swore that the famous Snake-eyed Randy Cole would solve all our problems.'

He swung the black around and dug his spurs in hard.

Cole quickly scrambled to his feet, all notions of retribution erased from his whirring brain.

'Hold up there, kid!' he called after the retreating back of the rider, whilst desperately trying to regain some measure of his shaken dignity. Finally managing to tree his boots, the farmer removed the worst of the reeking sludge from his person.

Reining up, Luke Bowdry swivelled around in the saddle then swung his mount back towards the pig farm. His pallid face had abandoned the look of supercilious mockery, assuming a forlorn cast.

For a youngster, his recent experiences on the Dirty Devil had forced on him an air of listless dejection. All the same, he was curious as to the stark divergence between his father's picturesque depiction of a one-time buddy, and the reality that now faced him across the smelly pig enclosure.

He sat upright in the saddle, waiting.

'What exactly do you want from me?' asked the farmer.

'My folks are in trouble and need help,' uttered the kid, a bleak tone invading his voice. 'Pa said you were the best there is with a six-shooter.'

Randy Cole hawked up a lump of black phlegm before responding to the look of contempt that had once again crept over the kid's pinched visage.

'That was a long time ago,' replied Cole pensively. 'My days as a mean-eyed gunslick are long since past.'

'Yep, I can sure see that,' smirked Luke re-establishing his scornful expression. 'Pa must have clear forgot that time marches onward. No way could an old crank like you handle Jute Farley and his gang of hardcases.'

Jute Farley!

Cole's eyes widened in shocked disbelief. Never had he thought to hear that detestable name uttered in his presence again.

After being released from the Colorado State Penitentiary following a painful ten years' hard labour, Randy had spent the next eighteen months hoping to hunt down the treacherous skunk. But Farley had covered his tracks well. And the search had proved futile.

In the end, Randy Cole had given up and bought the pig farm with proceeds from robberies that he had stashed away. It had proved to be a hard way to make a living. Profits no way matched the easy money he had pocketed and spent as a road agent. But he was too long in the tooth for resuming his old hell-raising ways, and it kept the starpackers off his back.

Jute Farley.

Just thinking on the critter's name set the blood pounding in his head. His ice-cold blue eyes misted over as the years rolled back. Once again he saw himself as the mean-eyed gunnie he had once been, leader of a gang of tearaways that no force of law and order had ever been able to tame.

Randy had always seen himself as the Jesse James of Colorado. The two outlaws were also similar in that a Judas had infiltrated their ranks and done for them both. In Jesse's case it had been a bullet in the back from Bob Ford. Luckily for Randy Cole, he had survived to fight another day. And he was determined that Jute Farley would pay the ultimate price for his betrayal of the gang.

Such a brazen assertion had proved to be words only.

Delving back through the turgid files of his memory, Randy had to dig deep to summon up the painful images that had led to his incarceration in the state penitentiary.

Eventually a hazy recollection lumbered into focus.

The year was 1873.

The Cole Gang had robbed a bank in the Colorado town of Gunnison. It had been a textbook robbery with no problems encountered. Not a shot had been fired, nor any resistance given. At the time,

Randy had figured it was his consummate planning that had ensured the smooth running of the operation. Never once had he suspected that the gang might have been set up.

Spurring out of town, the robbers headed back to their hideout in the mountain fastness of the Sawatch Range. The fact that they never caught sight of a posse on their tail ought to have rung the alarm bells.

Astute as ever, it was Clint Bowdry who pointed out this obvious fact.

'Seems kinda strange that we got away with this caper so easy like,' he remarked drawing his cayuse up beside that of the gang leader.

Cole shrugged off the outlaw's concern with a throwaway comment.

'You worry too much, Clint.'

He was too buoyed up having carried off a successful raid without firing a shot to accord that notion any serious thought.

It was an error of judgement that was to prove his undoing.

Following a holdup, Randy always insisted that the gang lie low in Deadman's Gulch for at least a week until the hue and cry died down.

But on this occasion he was persuaded, against his better judgement, into allowing Jute Farley to visit the nearest town of Crested Bute after only two days. The guy's reasoning that his cayuse's left front shoe needed replacing was met with a curt rebuttal from an ever sceptical Logan Hands.

'It would be just like this jigger to brag about the perfect job we've pulled,' commented Hands, jabbing a thumb at his confederate. The pair had always been at odds with each other. 'And then where would we be? Facin' a hefty term in the can.'

Farley speared him with a look of pure venom.

'It ain't for you to decide,' he hissed. 'So keep your lip buttoned.'

'All I'm sayin' is that you should stay put like the rest of us,' replied Hands.

Known as Shake by one and all, Hands was a born worrier. It stemmed from a particularly domineering wife who was forever finding fault with her henpecked husband. Much to his chagrin, she insisted on constantly reminding him of his lowly status as a dry goods clerk. Martha Hands had always harboured an ambition to rub shoulders with the more influential members of Durango's well-to-do community.

Soon after marrying Logan Hands she quickly realized that he was incapable of helping her attain such ambitions. That was the main reason why Shake had turned to crime. It paid well, and allowed him to escape from her acerbic tongue, sometimes for weeks on end.

He managed to explain away his periodic absences and acquisition of extra funds as a knack he had discovered of investing wisely in national stocks and bonds. Diplomatically, Martha chose not to question too closely the source of this most welcome route into high society.

Under normal circumstances Randy Cole would have agreed with the outlaw's remark and unequivocally vetoed Farley's suggestion. But the scheming jackal had made certain that Randy was well oiled before broaching the subject. In consequence, the boss's normally sharp brain was idling at a lethargic pace.

So he failed to heed Farley's malevolent glower, and chose to ignore the barbed rebuke from Shake Hands.

He did, however, recognize the need for some form of monitory comment.

'Just make sure you don't run off at the mouth,' Cole warned, jabbing a half-empty whiskey bottle at the outlaw. 'We don't want the law getting wind of our whereabouts.'

'Don't worry, boss,' asserted Farley with a wry smirk. 'Mum's the word. I'll be back afore you know it.'

'You sure this is the right thing to do?' Clint Bowdry felt obliged to interject in support of Shake's censure. 'We allus keep a low profile followin' a job.'

'My horse needs the services of a blacksmith,' reiterated Farley, trying to contain a rising sense of alarm. 'That is unless you've got the skills to do the job?'

Bowdry's response was an irritable grunt.

'Don't worry so much, Clint.' Cole's eyes were glassy, his words slurred as unwittingly he came to Farley's aid. 'And you too, Shake. Both of yuh are like a pair of old women sometimes. Ease back and have a drink.' A congenial smile creased his loose features as he handed the bottle to his sidekick. 'We're celebrating, ain't we? Wasn't this the slickest operation the gang ever pulled?'

'You're sure right there, boss,' agreed Stripes Gifford puffing hard on a thin quirly. 'Some fellas allus have to look on the black side.'

Bowdry couldnt deny that the job had been executed with methodical precision. Although being the gang's brakeman and imbued with a natural-born caution, he felt that this operation had gone rather too well. A vexing suspicion niggled at his brain that things weren't quite as they should be. Unfortunately, he couldn't quite put his finger on the nub of the matter.

Had the cynical outlaw taken note of the icy cast in Jute Farley's eye, he might well have had his answer. As it was, he shrugged and imbibed another liberal slug of hooch.

Farley jammed his hat on his bullet head and made for the door of the two-roomed log cabin. The sooner he was out of there and on the trail the better.

'You go easy on that nag,' warned Cole. 'Don't want him peggin' out on yuh.'

Farley merely nodded. His eagerness to leave passed without comment in the alcoholic fug that now enshrouded the cabin.

Once outside, the outlaw sighed with relief. Mounting up, he walked his cayuse the initial hundred yards away from the cabin before applying his spurs. The horse leapt forward displaying no hint that it was encumbered in any way.

But Farley had no intention of heading for Crested Butte.

Once clear of the hidden gulch where the unsuspecting gang members had resumed their celebrations, Farley headed west, back in the direction of Gunnison. His thin lips parted in a malign grin revealing teeth yellowed from too much baccy chewing.

The evil smirk was matched by a sudden grumbling of thunder rolling over the sawtooth peaks of the Sawatch. Large droplets of rain preceded a heavy and persistent downpour. But the uncomfortable soaking did nought to dampen the fleeing outlaw's thirsty resolve to betray his confederates.

Maverick Jones had been checking on the horses when he saw Farley spurring off down the trail. So he had not been cognizant of the outlaw's plea to leave the camp.

Shouldering through the cabin door, he shucked out of his slicker, then quickly voiced his concern.

'Where's Farley off to?'

'Gone to get a loose shoe fixed,' responded Bowdry peevishly.

Jones frowned.

'That roan of his seemed all right to me,' remarked the outlaw, injecting more than a modicum of cynical bite into the rejoinder. 'Galloped off slick as a squirrel up a tree.'

'Tell that to the boss,' interposed Logan Hands.

But Randy Cole had already succumbed to the

effects of a now empty whiskey bottle. The others failed to accord Jones's concern the attention it deserved. The whiskey had done its job well.

It was sunrise on the fourth day after the robbery. A weak sun nudged away the mist that clung to the valley sides. Pink and orange striations of early morn hesitantly surrendered to the dusky heat of day. But not before a posse of heavily armed men had secreted themselves around the outlaws' hideout.

Among their number was Jute Farley.

He had made it clear to the Sheriff of Gunnison that he would be acting in the capacity of a guide only. No way was he going to face down his ex-buddies and risk a dose of lead poisoning. Having secured the reward money for turning in the bandits, together with an affidavit signed by the state governor pardoning him for all past criminal activities, he quickly made himself scarce.

It was only when he was well on the north-bound trail heading for the Wyoming border that his ears picked up the distant crackle of gunfire. Farley tapped the bulging saddle-pack containing upwards of $3000. An easy smile played across the grizzled visage. Untainted by any hint of remorse or guilt, it swelled to a gleeful chortle as the treacherous Judas galloped off into a new day and a new life.

An early arrival at Deadman's Gulch in the Sawatch was meant to catch the gang at their most vulnerable.

It had succeeded.

The first intimation the outlaws had that Clint

Bowdry's gloomy predictions bore some semblance of truth was a blunt summons from without.

'You men inside the cabin. This is Sheriff Blake Masters from Gunnison. I have a warrant for your arrest on a charge of armed robbery.' He paused to let his message sink in. 'Come out with your hands high and nobody will get hurt. And don't think you can cut and run 'cos I got the place surrounded.'

The sheriff's guttural shout was intended to ensure that the slumbering incumbents of the cabin knew exactly how the land lay.

'Throw your weapons out and don't try anything stupid,' he repeated with a brusque intimation that any resistance would be futile.

The sluggish effects of a drink-induced slumber were quickly shaken loose as the outlaws snatched up rifles and pistols. Unlocking the shutters covering the open windows, they gingerly peered out at the muted light of early morn.

Bowdry instantly latched on to what had happened.

'It's that skunk, Farley,' he snarled. 'Betrayed us to the law.'

'I knew there was something funny about his itchin' to leave early,' concurred Shake Hands.

'So now we know,' added Maverick Jones, hugging the rosewood stock of his Winchester. 'Pity you fellas didn't listen when I told yuh there was nothin' wrong with his horse. There must be at least a dozen possemen out there.'

'No sense cryin' over spilt milk,' urged Randy

Cole, knowing it was his decision that had led to this shakedown. 'We need to think of a way out of this pickle.' As gang boss he should have exercised more control, been more solid in asserting his instincts which had always proven successful on previous occasions.

Now they were trapped. Stuck in this cabin like fish in a barrel.

None of the other gang members had voiced their disquiet at his inept decision. This was not the time for recriminations.

Even Concho Sterling had seen fit to keep his waspish comments under wraps. The youngest member of the gang, he was also the most debonair, hence the moniker he went by. Some gunslicks cut notches in their pistol grips. With Concho, it was silver discs affixed to his black Stetson hat band. At that moment they numbered six. Although Concho had notions of increasing his tally in the next few minutes.

Before the sheriff even finished issuing the ultimatum, Concho loosed off a half-dozen shots. A strident hoot of derision followed as a couple of high crowns lifted from exposed pates.

'That'll show the critters we ain't no easy touch,' he hollered.

The other outlaws quickly followed his lead. Gunfire erupted from all sides. The acrid stench of burnt cordite rapidly filled the small room. There was no way that the posse could winkle them out of the sturdy log cabin in a hurry.

But Randy knew that time was on the side of the posse. All they had to do was wait.

There was only a single pannikin of water in the cabin. Nowhere near enough for five men to slake their thirsts once the heat of day made its presence felt.

There was only one way out of this predicament. It was the reason he had chosen this particular abandoned miner's cabin as the gang's hideout.

Built up against a sheer rock face it meant that only a frontal assault could prevail. The door at the rear opened onto a narrow passage leading behind a clump of ponderosa pine and cottonwoods. It only afforded enough cover to provide an escape route for one man at a time crawling on his belly. But it was a chance. And one that he owed his men. Their horses were at the end of the line of trees, corralled in a side draw offset from the main gulch.

'Clint!' Randy called across to his close buddy, indicating for the grizzled outlaw to join him.

'How we gonna play this, Snake!' asked the older man, a hint of temerity in his voice as he thumbed fresh shells into the Henry repeater. 'Rush outside with all guns a-blastin' in a show of glory?'

The gang boss quickly spurned that notion.

'You got a death wish, Clint?' he asked, eyebrows raised. ' 'Cos I sure ain't.' He lowered his voice. 'No! We leave by the back door.' He then proceeded to explain his plan. 'Pass it on to the others while I check things out behind. I'll be the last out. We'll meet up at Frenchman's Creek on the north fork of the Green River in a week's time. We can divide up the loot there. Savvy?'

Bowdry responded with a brisk nod as he scuttled away to relay the boss's orders.

Twenty minutes later, only Clint Bowdry and Snake-eyed Randy Cole were left in the cabin. Both kept up a steady stream of fire for a few more minutes. During a lull, Randy turned to address his *compadre.*

'Your turn now, Clint,' he said.

Bowdry shook his head. A resolute cast was evident in his firm jawline.

'I ain't goin' any place without you,' he asserted forcefully.

Cole skewered his buddy with a mordant peeper before replying.

'Who's bossing this outfit?'

'You are.'

'Then you'll do exactly as I say.'

Bowdry was all set to argue the toss, but the gritty determination of his sidekick's dark frown elicited a brief nod of accord. He then handed over his own rifle.

'You'll be needing this more'n me.' Bowdry squeezed his pal's shoulder. 'It's fully loaded.'

A brief smile passed between the two outlaws.

'See you at Frenchman's Creek,' smiled Cole. He then jacked a fresh round into the breech and moved over to a window.

The gang boss managed to keep the posse at bay for a further half-hour before he was nailed by a ricochet that took him in the chest. He staggered back clutching at the grievous wound. Rivulets of blood dribbled between his fingers. No way could he hope to escape now.

But at least he'd given the rest of the boys time to make a clean getaway. With that thought, he grabbed hold of a grubby bed sheet and struggled across to the door.

Waving the once-white article as best he could without exposing himself, he announced in a cracked voice, 'OK, Masters, you win. Don't shoot. I'm coming out.'

THREE

RESURRECTION

Could this be his opportunity to finally rid the world of that treacherous sidewinder? Jute Farley had a lot to answer for. A fierce gleam played across Randy Cole's taut features.

He still had his guns. They'd been put in storage once he realized that time had moved on. Every so often though, he took out his rifle and did a spot of shooting. Rabbits and deer only these days. But it kept his hand in and helped fill the cooking pot. At least it afforded a change from pig meat.

But his pistols hadn't been used in a coon's age.

The notion that he was well past his best, no longer the cocky desperado of his youth, brought a mournful frown to the heavily contoured landscape of his face. Snake-eyed Randy Cole, ex-gunfighter and outlaw, knew deep down that he was too darned long in the tooth for riding the owlhoot trail.

This was the time when he should be taking things

easy. not living life on the edge. Once reckoned to be the fastest gunhand west of Denver, his callused mitts were now lumpy and scarred by age and hard manual toil.

Then again, he was being offered the chance to settle an old and niggling score. One last opportunity before the grim reaper came a-knocking on his door. It was not to be ignored.

He flexed his gun hand meaningfully. A little practice and he reckoned he could turn the years back. Just like swimming, you never lost the touch. At least, that was supposed to be the theory.

So who had sent this cocky young sprog to seek him out after all this time? Clearly it had to be someone who knew him from the old days.

He was intrigued enough to cut the youngster a loose rein.

'So what do they call you, kid?'

'The name's Luke.'

'Well then, Luke,' began Randy, trying to adopt a lighter tone. 'I think you'd better tell me who sent you and, more important, why?'

'My pa said that you could help us get rid of Jute Farley and his gang.' It was Luke's turn to assume a pensive grimace as he recalled the heinous threats made against his family. 'They shot him down when he couldn't meet the payments on the farm. And then Ma was. . . .'

All the youngster's previous bluster evaporated as he broke down. Shoulders heaving, he sobbed aloud, unable to contain the anguish that racked his body.

Randy hustled outside the pig enclosure and helped him down from the big horse. Arms protectively enfolding the thin frame, he took the boy inside the small farmhouse and sat him down. Only when he'd drunk some coffee and insisted the boy have something to eat did the farmer make any attempt to winkle out the brutal story.

Over the next hour, slowly and with numerous vacillations, the grim truth emerged like a picture from the Devil's paintbox.

Luke's mother had been taken to the barn while the boy was held by the other members of the gang. He did not understand the significance of what was happening. Only that when his mother emerged, her clothes were torn, a tortured look of anguish ravaged her once lovely features. Soon after, her tormentor appeared, a lurid grin pasted across his ugly face.

The kid might not realize it, but Randy knew exactly what had occurred in the barn that black day. His hackles rose at the thought of what this woman had suffered at the hands of none other than Jute Farley.

She did not speak for three whole days.

That was when she told Luke to go and find Snake-eyed Randy Cole. When he had asked where the guy lived, all she could tell him was that the legendary gunfighter had always nursed a hankering to settle down at Hole-in-the-Wall in Wyoming territory.

So who were these people who knew so much about his past?

Randy sucked in a deep breath. A roll of thunder

echoed down the valley. The pregnant sow emitted a harsh oink in reply.

Crunch time had arrived.

'Has yer pa got a name, Luke?'

Time seemed to hang suspended as the words formed on the boy's lips.

'Clint Bowdry.'

Randy's jaw dropped.

Now he knew the truth of the matter. His old partner in crime was in trouble and needed help. And Jute Farley was a principal player in the sordid affair. He stood up and ambled over to a shelf upon which resided a jug of home-distilled moonshine. Resting the heavy earthen container in the crook of his left arm, he imbibed a liberal slug. He needed it after what the kid had just divulged.

Knowing that his one-time best buddy and partner-in-crime was in dire straits changed everything. No way could he fail to respond. Without any hesitation, he reached behind and opened a large oak chest.

Removing a faded oilskin bag he unwrapped the greased cloth and gingerly played his fingers over the smooth black leather gunbelt. The carved ivory butt of a Colt Peacemaker protruded from a cut-down holster. Slivers of light reflected off the polished nickel-plated barrel. It was many a long day since it had been fired in anger.

Deftly sliding the revolver from its housing, he spun the perfectly balanced weapon on his middle finger. Flicking the pistol into the air he caught it expertly in his left hand before continuing the display of manual dexterity. Right to left and back again.

Luke could only stare open-mouthed. Maybe this guy wasn't such a has-been after all.

Randy smiled at the youngster's awed response, pleased that he still had the wherewithal.

'The Border Shift,' he announced, a wry smirk crinkling the deep fissures of his soiled visage. 'Once learnt, never forgotten.' The grin widened. Randy was enjoying the feel of the cold steel in his hands.

It had been a long time.

'I see you favour the Navy Colt,' he said having noted the youngster's choice of firearm when he first arrived at the homestead.

'Pa gave it to me when Farley and his gang started causing trouble. He taught me how to fire and hit the target on the draw.'

'Your pa always was a good shot,' replied Cole. Then, grasping the ivory butt of his own .45, he offered it to the youngster. 'Fancy trying this fella out for size?'

Luke reached to take hold of the tendered revolver. But he never got the chance. In the blink of an eye, he was staring down the yawning snout of the blued barrel.

Cole found the kid's startled surprise hilarious. Slapping his thigh, he vented forth a raucous hoot of laughter.

'Don't you worry none, young shaver,' he cackled, 'It ain't loaded.' Simmering down, the ex-gunsel replaced the pistol in its tooled leather housing, patting it affectionately like you would a faithful old wolfhound.

'That trick was taught me by the guy who reckons he invented it.'

He then proceeded to relate the legendary meeting. 'One time back in '72 Curly Bill Brocius was causing a ruckus down in Tombstone. When Marshal White tried to arrest him, Curly pretended to be cowed by the lawdog's intimidating manner. Putting on a hang-dog expression, and curling his lip, he slowly took out his pistol and made to hand it over. Then, cool as you please, he pulled that stunt on him.' A wistful cast softened the old guy's features. 'Sure wish I'd been there to see that.'

'Did Curly manage to get away?' asked a gaping Luke Bowdry. Randy had clearly begun to impress the youngster. He intended making the most of it.

'Sure did. And that very same dodge has gotten me out of a few scrapes I can tell you.'

'Will you teach me, Mr Cole?' Luke's puppy-dog brown eyes held the old outlaw in their hypnotic gaze. 'I'm a fast learner.'

Randy didn't doubt it. The kid was smart. And he was tempted. It was a long time since anybody had taken heed of what Randy Cole had to say. He peered into the big round peepers and inwardly sighed. If things had worked out differently, he could have had a son just like Luke Bowdry. At that moment, Randy felt a pang of jealousy towards his old sidekick.

The musing reverie was instantly shrugged aside.

Clint Bowdry was in trouble. And it was a long ride back to Utah.

'Maybe, kid,' he drawled slipping the gun back into its holster. 'When this business has been sorted.'

It was just after sun-up the next day when the two riders left the pig farm.

The threatening rainstorm had thankfully moved off to the north. Dark clouds contrasted with the golden glow now expelling the mantle of night on their right hand. Pointing their mounts down valley, they headed south-west between the surging turrets of red sandstone that enclosed the natural stronghold of Hole-in-the-Wall.

Late the previous afternoon, the pigman had ridden over to secure the co-operation of his nearest neighbour in running the farm while he was away. Big Nose Jim Parrot was another ex-con who had chosen to reside in this sector of the Big Horn mountains.

Wild and far removed from the nearest sheriff's office, Hole-in-the-Wall was also a regular thoroughfare for numerous outlaw gangs who needed to lie low for a spell. The permanent residents were not averse to providing help and sustenance to any passing brigands, for a suitable remuneration, of course.

As they rode, Luke peered about him marvelling at the sumptuous feast that Mother Nature had fashioned with her own peculiar brand of eccentricity. He had been unable to appreciate his surroundings on the frightening trail north. He cast a quick glance at the stoic profile of the grizzled hardcase riding beside him.

Now that Randy's life had a new purpose, old habits were resurrected. Searching eyes diligently probed every mound and trough. Snake eyes! Hard and menacing yet strangely solid and dependable.

The youngster smiled to himself. He felt comfortable, secure in the knowledge that everything would turn out right in the end now that the hard-boiled gunfighter was on side.

The rose-tinted image of youth? Maybe. Only time would tell.

For the first two hours they rode in silence.

It was Randy Cole who made the opening gambit.

'We'll be following the old outlaw trail south through Brown's Park and along the Green River,' he informed his young companion. 'Ought to take no more'n ten days if we press on at a good lick.'

'That all?' exclaimed a surprised Luke Bowdry. 'Took me almost a month to find your pitch.'

'That's 'cos you only had a vague notion of my whereabouts.' At that moment he swung his horse towards a dark lump poking above the rolling ocean of gently swaying grass. 'See that?' Randy pointed towards the approaching landmark.

Luke had to strain his eyes to focus onto what was in effect merely a blackened tree stump.

'What is it?' he asked.

'The post office!' replied his confederate barely able to contain the wily grin that threatened to bend his features out of alignment.

The kid peered at him as if his new partner was crazy. Randy's answer was a conspiratorial, 'You'll see!'

Another five minutes and they drew rein beside the hollow stump. Randy leaned down, delving inside the dark interior. Extracting a single brown envelope his straw eyebrows lifted in surprise on perceiving his own name written on the front. The elegant sweep of the lettering suggested that the sender was female.

Curiousity combined with a blend of mystery and concern removed any trace of humour from his face.

Who could have sent such a missive?

There was only one way to find out. Stepping down, he handed the reins to Luke and without a word moved off while gingerly extracting the two sheets of writing paper inside.

After perusing the contents, his broad shoulders slumped, a saturnine cloud settling across the weathered features. Hooded eyes narrowed as the full import of what he had just read began to sink in.

Luke sensed that something was amiss. The letter had clearly not brought happy tidings to the recipient.

'What's wrong, Randy?' he enquired.

The gunfighter appeared not to hear. He moved further away keeping his back to the youngster so he could not perceive the woeful presence now haunting the gunfighter's thoughts. In truth, Randy needed time to absorb the awesome implications of what the brief communication had unleashed.

He read the letter for a second time.

Dear Randy,
I hope that you will receive this letter before my son Luke finds you. Sit down before you read it. There are things to be said that might prove hard for you to accept.

When you failed to turn up at Frenchman's Creek following the bank job at Gunnison, the gang split up. Only later did I learn that you had been caught and sent to prison. By then I had also discovered that I was pregnant. Clint knew that the child had to be yours, but he was willing to accept the responsibility. We married before it showed to avoid the usual gossip. Even though my love for you will never die, I have always respected Clint and come to love him over the years.

He has been shot and badly wounded by Jute Farley and you are the only person who can help. Farley and his gang are working for a new land agent who has threatened to evict us from the farm. Clint, as you know, was always a stubborn cuss and refused to play ball. He didn't stand a chance. The day after Luke left the farm he passed away. I can only hope you break it to him gently.

Please do not think that I betrayed our love. You know how it is for unmarried mothers in the West. I ask one last favour which is that Luke must never learn the identity of his real father. He revered Clint, and that must be upheld at all costs.

Farley has already forced his attentions on me. He

wants a willing partner, but I can only keep stalling his loathsome mauling for so long. If you still value what we once had, please come quickly.

Yours,

Jan Bowdry, Mrs

All the sorrows of the world pressed down onto Randy's hunched back.

She was right. This revelation was hard to accept. Snake-eyed Randy Cole, hard-boiled criminal and scourge of the law, reduced to a quivering wreck.

His legs felt like jelly forcing him to sit down on the old tree stump. Distant memories of what might have been flooded back with a vengeance. Tears etched a winding trail down the seamed corridors of his face, dribbling onto the letter and smearing the black ink. His only true love had married his best buddy who had now been killed at the hands of a treacherous dog. And not only that, he had a son he could not acknowledge.

Such momentous revelations took some heeding.

It was the sight of Jan's written plea dissolving before his watery eyes that finally jerked the old outlaw from his reverie and back to the present. Here was a dilemma that could not be ignored.

Out the corner of a tear-filled eye, a dark shadow emerged from the haunting dreamworld: Luke Bowdry . . . his son . . . sitting there, waiting, pondering. Maybe a little fearful as the boy weighed up the import of this sudden change of demeanour.

Randy could not allow his own personal feelings to

cloud his judgement. He quickly shook off the leaden torpor and stood up, squaring his broad shoulders.

Luke edged his mount closer.

'You sure there ain't nothing wrong?' pressed the anxious youngster.

'Nothing for you to fret over,' the ex-robber asserted a touch too emphatically. 'Just a report from the pig breeders' association about a fall in the price of meat.'

Pushing the letter inside his sheepskin jacket, Randy hoisted himself into the saddle and spurred off. A somewhat bewildered Luke Bowdry followed at a distance.

FOUR

SCALP MAN

The only incident worthy of note on the trail south occurred on the evening of the seventh day. Incident was understating what could have resulted in dire consequences for Randy Cole's continued good health. Indeed, what happened on the banks of the Green River could be construed as a major threat to life and limb.

The two riders had made camp for the night at a point where the Big Brush merges with the Green just south of the Utah line. Luke had gone some distance downstream to find an ideal spot where he could lie down and study the swirling flow in order to catch a pair of brown trout for their supper. The tickle and grab method was a task that required infinite patience, which Luke had in abundance.

Back at the campsite, Randy had just brewed a jug of coffee when his ears picked up an alien noise. It hailed from the edge of the tree cover surrounding the open glade where they had set up camp some fifty yards back from the river-bank.

'Hallo the camp!' called out a gruff voice from the far side of the clearing. This was the usual manner by which strangers approached a lone camp in the wilderness if they didn't want their heads blown off. And it was expected that hospitality would be willingly given. 'Any chance of joining you? That coffee smells mighty good.'

Randy's body stiffened. His hand rested on the butt of his revolver.

'How many are you?' he hollered back, a curt edge to his reply. He was taking no chances.

'Only the one,' came back the response. 'Just a lone rider like your good self heading south from Rock Springs.'

'Show yourself!' ordered Randy. 'And keep your mitts high where I can see 'em.'

A heavily bearded jigger with long grey hair broke from the tree cover. Holding his arms wide to indicate he meant no harm, the man came forward. He was clad in greasy, well-worn buckskins with a large eagle feather stuck in his coonskin cap. He didn't appear to be armed. But Randy knew that nobody in his right mind travelled this wild land without some form of protection.

Still, the guy didn't appear to pose any threat.

The gunfighter relaxed.

'Sit down for a spell, stranger,' he said filling up a mug and handing it to the man. 'You're sure welcome to share my vittles if'n you don't mind trail grub.'

'Much obliged,' replied the heavy-set man.

Sipping the steaming brew, he eyed his benefactor across the dancing embers of the camp-fire. Deftly rolling a quirly, he lit up and drew hard on the thin tube, all the while studying Randy.

Then, drawing back his thick lips into a shifty leer, the newcomer said tightly, 'I appreciate the offer, mister, but there's some'n else that I've taken a notion to rather than yer vittles.'

The narrowed eyes, hooded and with a malevolent gleam, should have warned Randy that this jigger was up to no good. He had let his guard drop. After all, what trouble could one lone jasper offer to a gunfighter like Randy Cole?

But the cool snaked-eyed regard of old had been blunted.

As a result, he failed to hear the guy's confederate sneak up behind and slug him across the head. Randy never knew what hit him. He keeled over without uttering a sound.

'Now weren't that a cinch, eh, Wilks?' guffawed the second man addressing his partner while discarding the heavy wooden club.

'Yuh can sure say that agin,' chuckled Wilks, booting the unconscious man in the ribs.

'Easier than takin' candy from a baby,' observed the slugger who went by the handle of Mancos.

'That paint mare of his will do me fine, now that old Betsy has given up the ghost,' announced Wilks, walking over and stroking the nervous animal on its muzzle. 'You and me's gonna be partners,' he simpered.

'If'n you're havin' the cayuse,' declared Mancos vehemently, 'then I'm takin' this turkey's fancy gun rig.' He eyed the tooled-leather shellbelt and its custom-made firearm with greedy yearning. 'Ain't ever had me a hogleg like this afore.' Hooking out the ancient .31 Whitney from his belt, Mancos flung it away in disgust, then bent down to unfasten the belt from around Randy's waist.

Meanwhile, some two miles away, Luke had finally managed to snatch his second trout trom the surging waters of the Green. By this time, evening was laying down its shadowy cloak as the fading sun drifted down behind the Wasatch Mountains to the west. A cooling breeze stirred the dwarf willows along the river's edge.

Stuffing the catch into his saddle-bag, Luke mounted the black and made his way back towards the campsite. A faint glow from the fire upstream lit his way. It was only when he was within hailing distance that he heard raised voices. Surely the old guy hadn't succumbed to chatting to himself. Luke smiled at the notion.

But the smug grin was quickly erased from the smooth profile of his face. There was more than one voice and both displayed a gruffer more guttural inflection, not the easy Texan drawl he had come to know.

Nor was this a sociable confab between trail buddies.

Something was wrong.

Stepping down from his mount, he hustled quickly

to the edge of the clearing. What he perceived elicited a sharp intake of breath. An icy shiver scuttled down his spine.

Randy Cole was laid out on the ground. There was no way of telling if he was dead. Certainly there was no sign of any movement from Luke's stricken partner.

Both of the skunks had finished ransacking the camp and were preparing to leave when one of them drew a knife. It was heavy-bladed, curved and at least ten inches in length, glinting evilly in the light cast by the flames.

The bearded owner grinned at his confederate.

'The Utes pay in gold for white-eyes' scalps,' he purred wickedly. 'This fellas blond locks should keep us in hooch for some time to come.'

He moved across to the prostrate form.

Luke knew that he had to do something. And quick!

He looked down. The Navy had somehow appeared in his hand.

The wicked blade lifted. Its razored edge was aimed at the thick blond locks clutched in the butcher's hand.

Another few seconds and it would be too late.

Luke dragged the hammer back to full cock and fired. His aim was high, but the loud report was enough to delay the projected scalping. Mancos turned his head to face the surprise attacker. His mouth gaped wide.

The second bullet was much more successful, removing half the critter's face. Blood and gore sprayed from the fatal wound.

Acidic bile filled Luke's throat. His stomach lurched uncontrollably. Killing a man was nothing like hunting rabbits. And he would have thrown up had not the immediate thought registered that over to his left, Wilks was even now drawing his own weapon.

A savage growl disgorged from the bushwhacker's twisted maw.

Once again, the cap 'n ball pistol was brought to bear. But at this crucial moment, it failed. An icy panic gripped the youngster's entrails. Desperately, he tried to free the jammed mechanism.

Wilks let out a howl of crazed delight. The manic hollering soon dissolved into a truculent snarl. This kid had gunned down his partner and had every intention of repeating the process if he was given the chance. The hardcase had no intention of allowing that course of action to come to fruition.

Mean, piggy eyes narrowed to thin slits. Stepping forward, he took aim.

'Here's where yuh get yours, kid,' he growled angrily, as a fresh notion dawned in his warped brain. 'Now I've gotten me two scalps, not to mention a couple of fine cayuses.'

The hammer ot the skunk's old army Remington snapped back.

Luke was transfixed, his whole body stunned into immobility.

The sharp crack of a pistol split the ether. But it was Wilks who staggered back, arms akimbo. A red patch quickly spread across his chest as a second shot rang out. The man seemed to pirouette like a ballet dancer as the bullet ploughed into his left shoulder. It was the third shot that finally shut the lights down permanently.

Randy Cole's leather hat with its thick snakeskin band had cushioned the heavy blow to his skull. He had been stunned into oblivion, but only temporarily. The heavy sound of gunfire had nudged his swimming brain back into life.

And only just in time.

Observing his companion resting on one elbow, smoking revolver clutched in his hand, released the pent-up tension in Luke's guts. Not to mention the contents of his stomach which spewed out in a gurgling rush. He staggered over to the edge of the glade, retching violently.

Randy considered it prudent to leave his young partner alone to settle both mind and body. Coming to terms with the grim realities of life in the remote wilderness of a lawless frontier was no picnic. In the meantime, the gunfighter took a gander at the two lowlife trail bums who had ambushed him.

The critter known as Wilks was unknown to him. Moving across to the mangled corpse of the other bushwhacker, his nose wrinkled in disgust as he eyed the grisly remains. A frown etched Randy's broad forehead as he took a closer look. A low whistle hissed from between pursed lips.

'Well, whadya know?' he muttered to himself. Even with half the bum's ugly face in ruins, he couldn't fail to recognize an old associate. 'What in the name of

Judas are you doing in these parts, Mancos?'

The outlaw had ridden with Jute Farley before the treacherous varmint had joined up with the Cole Gang. So was it merely a coincidence that these two panhandlers had been heading in the same direction? Or was there some more sinister reason for them just happening along this trail?

A quick search of the outlaw's clothing revealed the answer. It was a telegraph wire sent to Rock Springs the previous week. It read: *M. Good job on offer Monticello. Excellent pay. JF.*

A shifty character like Mancos would have cottoned on to the import of the message straight away.

And so did Randy Cole.

Jute Farley was getting a sizeable gang together. He looked as if he clearly had more than just the scaring off of a few farmers in mind.

Luke chose that moment to emerge from the bushes. His face was whiter than an Arctic Fox as he shuttled across the open space. Randy slipped the wire inside his coat. No need to complicate matters.

It was some time later after they had shifted their camp to a more agreeable site, and were eating supper beside a gratifying blaze that Randy thanked his young partner for saving his hair, and his life.

Luke shrugged. 'One good turn deserves another,' the lad observed.

Coffee and the delicious fried trout had helped settle churning guts. But Luke's voice remained flat, devoid of emotion as he stared hard into the flickering tongues of orange. Even under the heat from the fire, his face still conveyed a waxy pallor.

Luke Bowdry had never killed a human being before.

His confederate recognized the fact that for a twelve-year-old boy, it must have been a grievous experience.

'You did what had to be done,' he averred, resting a consoling hand on the boy's shoulder. 'There ain't no shame in that.'

Had a brutalizing occurrence like this brought them closer together? Or had it made the boy aware of what life in the company of a gunfighting man had to offer? And that he wanted no part of such a liaison. Was this the time to inform the boy of his real father's identity! And would that knowledge send him over the edge?

Questions, questions! But no answers.

Randy was in a quandary of indecision.

And so the moment passed.

The hot sun blazed down from a cloudless azure sky. Two buzzards circled overhead, drifting effortlessly on the shimmering thermals. A week had passed since the brutal incident on the Green River. And, like everything else in life, time was a great healer. Especially where a young mind was involved. It wasn't that Luke had forgotten, just that events had shifted forward. And the original reason for his journey north was now paramount in his thoughts.

The two riders had arrived at what appeared to be

a solid rock wall. Round the next bend, however, a notched gap in the Orange Cliffs revealed itself. Known as Heaven's Gate, it was a short cut that Randy had used in his outlaw days. It effectively reduced their journey time by two days.

Picking a zig-zagged course down the far side of the pass on a trail no wider than a single mount was a hair-raising experience. A tight smile eased aside Randy's lips as the bizarre speculation crossed his mind. Here he was going to assist the wife of a deceased old buddy in the company of his new-found son. Nobody could invent such an unlikely turn of events.

Below, the valley of the Dirty Devil opened out to reveal a thin strip of rich grazing land, the first they had encountered since entering the labyrinth of deep canyonlands that characterized most of eastern Utah.

It brought a lump to his throat. This was the place that Clint had chosen to make his home in companionable harmony with Randy's old flame, and his son.

They had been riding for two hours when Luke reined in his mount.

'The farm is just over that rise,' he announced in a cracked voice, heavily laced with fearful trepidation.

FIVE

ASHES TO ASHES

Pausing while the boy recovered his composure, Randy empathized with the starkly bleak conjectures that were doubtless churning around inside Luke's head. Not knowing was the worst kind of torment.

The gunfighter slowly eased his mount forward up the rise. Cresting the brow, he halted abruptly, staring open-mouthed at the sight that met his bulging eyes. Shock registered across his gaunt features. There was no way of disguising the bitter reality.

Luke came up beside him.

There, not more than a quarter-mile distant, in what should have been an idyllic shady hollow, lay the charred remains of the Bowdry farm. Black oak beams pierced the air like the bones of some long extinct dinosaur. Wisps of smoke rose from the desolate heap of ash indicating that the heinous act had only recently been perpetrated.

Maybe somebody down there was still alive.

A contorted howl of anguish akin to that of a raving banshee emerged from the boy's ravished soul. It sounded like nothing Randy had ever heard before. Luke dug his boot heels into the black, driving the beast downhill towards the burnt husk that had once been his home.

Randy followed at a more restrained pace, trying to get his head round the corollaries this obscene tableau conjured up.

Luke leapt from the saddle, scurrying in and out of the ruined hulk, searching, praying for some intimation that his parents might still be alive.

'Pa! Are you there! Ma! It's me, Luke.'

Scrabbling amongst the wreckage, desperate for a miracle, his pleadings grew ever weaker and more forlorn as the devastating realization took a hold of his fevered imagination.

His parents were dead.

Then he noticed a cross over in the far corner of the small garden that his mother had assiduously cultivated. It was bent over, leaning at an angle. He frowned. It had not been there when he left to go in search of Randy Cole.

Forcing himself to his feet, Luke staggered across to the small grave and read aloud the epitaph carved into the wooden cross.

'Here lies Clinton Joseph Bowdry, a loving husband and father.'

Clearly, the man he still thought of as his father had not recovered from the gunshot wound. Yet another shock for his traumatized mind to cope with.

Where would it all end?

It was obvious that the sacred resting place had been foully desecrated. A myriad hoofprints indicated that horsemen had trampled across the grave, vilely besmirching his father's memory.

Luke beat his small fists against the hard-packed earth.

'They ain't gonna get away with this, Pa,' he cried, tears coursing down his cheeks. 'If it's the last thing I do, I'll hunt down these dirty skunks and make them pay for what they've done to us.'

Randy stood to one side, hat clutched in his hands. This was not the time for meaningless words of comfort. What solace could a young boy take from having his whole world destroyed?

Jute Farley had a lot to answer for.

But uppermost in the gunfighter's mind was the fate of Jan Bowdry. Although he had only been able to make a cursory examination of the burnt remains, there was no sign of any other body amidst the chaos.

For that he was grateful.

So what had become of her?

The obvious scenario was that Farley had got tired of being put off by Jan's delaying tactics. Now that she was a widow woman, it seemed clear his baser instincts had triumphed. No longer able to accept the frustrating of his carnal appetites, the bastard had carried her off to his hideaway.

He peered at Luke. The boy had ceased crying. There were no more tears. He just knelt beside the sullied grave, head bowed. A glassy look of shocked horror had stunned his brain into immobility.

Randy took the opportunity to make a more thorough search of the ruins.

An hour later, he was certain that Jan Bowdry was not there.

In the meantime the boy did not appear to have moved a muscle. The day was fast calling time. Shadows crept across the yard heralding the imminent approach of eventide.

Randy knew that it was his responsibility to precipitate a move. Food and a good night's sleep might help to nudge the boy out of his comatose reaction to the awful blow he had received. During his foray, he had managed to salvage some tins from the destruction. At least they offered something more than the trail grub they had survived on for the last ten days.

His attempt to create some semblance of order from the chaos was met with a blank, spiritless regard of apathy.

'You gotta eat something, boy,' he stressed pressing a plate of stew into Luke's hands. 'If only to keep your strength up. I need to find you someplace to stay while I go after Farley and his minions.'

That was the moment Luke chose to elbow aside the dark cloud that had enveloped his broken spirit. An iron-hard glower of utter loathing chilled the gunfighter to his very core. How could a youngster such as Luke harbour such black thoughts? Yet however macabre and disturbing, he recognized that it was an understandable response knowing what the boy had suffered.

'Don't you figure for a minute, Mr Cole, that I aim to sit by and do nothing to bring these critters to justice.' Luke's tone was measured and precise. 'Whatever you intend doing, I want to be a part of it.'

Randy attempted to dissuade the boy from such a dangerous undertaking. Being of tender years, Luke had no idea of the hazards involved. But the kid was adamant. Randy's tanned features broke into a knowing smile.

'Just like your old man,' he clucked, shaking his head. 'Stubborn as a mule, with as many brains.' For the first time, Luke's mouth crinkled in a brief suggestion of a grin. 'We'll talk about it in the morning.'

'I won't feel any different,' ejaculated the boy firmly.

'We'll see.'

In the event it was sheer exhaustion that finally sent the boy off into the land of Nod.

During the night, Randy's own sleep was constantly disturbed by his son's nightmarish outbursts. It was heartrending for the old outlaw who found these unfamiliar emotions difficult to handle. All he could do to ease the boy's distress was bathe the sweating face with a damp cloth. It came as a relief that eventually, he did succumb to the gunfighter's ham-fisted ministrations.

Morning loomed bright and cheerful. A cactus wren ushered in the new day with breezy disregard for the rampant havoc of its surroundings.

Unable to get back to sleep, Randy had surfaced in company with the false dawn, and a particularly vocal rooster, who appeared to sense that all was not well on the Bowdry homestead. The gunfighter had managed to commandeer some potatoes unearthed from the vegetable plot which he tossed into the fire to bake.

When Luke eventually got up, a jaundiced eye followed the unappetizing culinary preparations of his confederate. Then his gaze lit upon the ravaged desecration of his home. Any thoughts he had of satisfying the inner boy instantly dissolved in a rush of undisguised yearning for revenge.

Levering himself up onto one elbow, he met the eye of his partner, then waved aside the proffered dish.

Randy could see from the boy's tightly drawn features that he was still hell bent on riding a vengeance trail.

'It's gonna be one helluva nasty undertaking, son.' The gunfighter laid heavy emphasis on the significance of his advice in the hope of discouraging the youngster from his blinkered resolve. 'People are gonna get killed and I don't wanna be responsible for some young mossy horn getting hisself shot up.'

'I ain't about to change my mind,' Luke avowed with a solid conviction. It was clear that no amount of persuasion was going to deter the boy from the grim business of hunting down his father's killers and rescuing his mother. 'And you'd be wasting your time to even try. Anyway, I can't expect you to do my dirty work for me.' The boy's reasoning was cool and implacable. 'And don't be forgetting that you owe me for saving your bacon on the Green.'

'So there's nothing I can do that'll change your mind?' Randy made one final attempt at dissuasion.

The boy regarded him with a leaden expression that implied that nothing short of a meeting with the Grim Reaper would sway his determination. As a further testament, he grabbed a hold of his rifle, jammed the stock into his right shoulder and squinted along the barrel. Two seconds later a leaping jack-rabbit tumbled head over heels and lay still.

'And I can use a long gun as well,' he said, challenging the older man to deny his contention. 'And not only to bag a real breakfast.'

Randy knew when he was beaten. His broad shoulders lifted in a sigh of resignation.

'At least we now have some fresh meat,' he pressed. 'You're gonna need it if'n it's a manhunt you're intent on pursuing.'

Luke had the sense to recognize the truth of his partner's remark. A half-hour later, the rabbit had been skinned and cooked. He accepted the plate and eagerly devoured the tasty comestibles.

Over the meal, Randy made a proposal.

'You'll be needing a decent sidearm to back up that Sharps. Something that ain't too heavy. And I've got just the thing.' He tried to inject a hint of confidence into the remark. However, an uneasy feeling of grave misgiving was evident in the hard set of his gritty features. He forced it aside. Then, with poignant emphasis, added, 'One that don't jam!'

The gunfighter stood up and ambled across to his saddle-pack and delved inside. Removing an oilcloth bag, he produced a shiny, nickel-plated revolver with a bone handle engraved with the initials RC.

'And now is as good a time as any to make certain you have the makings.'

With deft precision he twirled the small gun on his middle finger, flipping it from hand to hand before tossing it at the startled youth.

'Catch!'

Luke easily managed to prevent the handsome weapon tumbling into the dust.

'You learn fast, kid,' chuckled Randy.

'I have a good teacher.' The boy returned the grin with an abashed smile of his own. It was the first pinch of levity that had passed between the two unlikely confederates since they had met two weeks before.

'Where's the hammer?' frowned the boy, gingerly eyeing the small gun.

'Don't need one 'cos it's double-action,' posited the gunfighter. 'Just keep pulling the trigger and it'll fire. Much better than that old cap 'n ball Navy that Clint gave you. Sure, they were fine weapons in their time. But these days you need something less cumbersome. The Colt .41 Lightning is ideal. And it won't snag on your clothes when a fast draw is needed.' He handed over a box of shells. 'Go and have a practice.'

'Gee thanks, Mr Cole,' beamed Luke, thumbing

the cartridges into the loading slot. 'I much appreciate this.'

'Just make sure you can shoot straight and true,' underlined Randy with staunch vigour, 'when the time comes.'

As the boy was turning away, eyes locked onto his much-prized acquisition, Randy called him back.

'Now that we's partners,' he averred effecting a serious mien, 'maybe you should start calling me Randy.' He would have preferred *Pa* but that was out of the question. He had to respect Jan Bowdry's wishes.

Luke considered the suggestion before replying.

'How about Snake?' he grinned. 'Sounds a heap more menacing. Then I can threaten them skunks with a deadly bite if'n they don't surrender.'

'Fangs a bunch, partner,' he responded with mock umbrage. As it happened, Randy couldn't have been more delighted. That was how his best buddy, and the boy's adopted father, had always addressed him.

Taking Randy's casual smirk as a nod of accord, the boy scooted off intent on familiarizing himself with his new yet deadly companion. Meantime, Randy was musing over how he was going play things from here on. He rolled a smoke and allowed the calming effect of the tobacco to focus his thoughts.

The main objective was to discover where Jute Farley was holed up.

From what the boy had told him, Jethro Tindale seemed his best bet to furnish that sort of information. The grasping land agent was bound to know the whereabouts of his chief enforcer. If he proved reluctant to divulge the gang's location, Randy would have to indulge in some more forthright means of persuasion.

He smiled at the notion. Over the years he had learned a few tricks in that department and had every confidence the desk-bound varmint would reveal all. Knuckleheads like that had no backbone. They always employed others to do their dirty work.

Skunks like Jute Farley!

SIX

THE CHAMELEON

It was mid morning when the two partners quit the shattered homestead that had been Luke's home.

'There's only two things that'll see me back here,' commented the boy after taking a last bleak-eyed look around the grim site.

Randy was intrigued.

'And what might they be, young fella?'

'To rebuild the place and start up again . . . or!' – an icy shiver rippled down the gunfighter's spine as the boy met his gaze with a blank, cold-blooded stare – 'in a pine box to lie beside my pa.'

'Don't you be talking that way,' chided the gunfighter with more confidence than he felt. 'Clint sent you to find me 'cos he knew I'd do the business. And that's just what I aim to do.' He patted the boy on the back, and with a cheeky smile added, 'With your help, of course. It's gonna be Jute Farley pushing up the daisies when we find the critter, not you or me. Got that?'

The boldly dealt assurance had the effect of returning some colour to the boy's pallid complexion. His reaction was a ready nod. It was just what he wanted to hear.

Early afternoon found them cresting a low rise. Below them were laid out the cluster of buildings that made up the county seat of Monticello.

Randy drew to a halt.

'Best we enter the town separately,' he ruminated thoughtfully. 'Don't want any nosy jasper getting too curious, especially a tin star.'

Luke offered a shrewd nod of understanding. 'How we gonna play this, Snake?'

The gunfighter suppressed a smile. Luke was deadly serious.

'You head down and pick up this list of supplies,' he said, handing the boy a note and some silver dollars. 'I'm gonna pay this Tindale jigger a visit. Pretend that I'm one of them bushwhackers we left back on the Green and that I want directions to Farley's camp. They'll no doubt be expected. And Tindale's bound to know where the gang's hiding out. If it ain't too far, we can meet up back here in say' – he flipped out a gold pocket watch – 'one hour. Then we go manhunting. And remember,' he cautioned with an admonitory wag of his index finger, 'we don't know each other.'

He gave Luke ten minutes before following at a gentle trot down the shallow grade. Monticello snuggled comfortably on the leeward slopes of the Elk Ridge Mountains. Protected from the predominant westerly winds that had carved the orange sandstone into a series ot contorted shapes, it had grown up at a meeting of trails – north/south linking the Green River country with Arizona, and eastward to the silver mining camps of Colorado.

There was talk of a possible railroad extension from Durango, but thus far the project had been nothing but hot air.

Not wishing to draw undue attention to himself, Randy hunched into his jacket and tugged down the broad brim of his leather hat to conceal his features. Nobody paid him any heed. Just another down-at-heel drifter passing through. Nonetheless, it paid to err on the side of caution.

He had never visited Monticello before. In the old days, the gang had never figured it had anything to offer in the way of financial inducement.

That situation appeared to have changed. The town certainly gave the outward impression of being prosperous. Even to the extent of enjoying street lighting. Warily scanning the buildings on either side of the main drag, Randy's snake-eyed scrutiny quickly spotted the one he was seeking.

There was no mistaking the imposing office of the Green River Development Agency. The large sign made certain that the company enjoyed a prime location at the centre of things. It was one of only two brick-built structures, the other being the Utah State Bank. Even the sheriff's office was only fashioned from adobe.

Jethro Tindale would appear to be an important dignitary, a conniving weasel able to hide his nefarious dealings behind a respectable persona. Randy was looking forward to making his acquaintance.

Slowing his mount to a gentle walk provided the opportunity to gather his thoughts. Playing the part of a hired gunhand was no problem for an ex-hold-up man. He needed to tease out the information that he might well be expected to know. Tindale no doubt closed his eyes to the repellent details of how the acreage along the Dirty Devil was being obtained – just so long as the company acquired possession without getting its hands dirty. And that's where the hiring of Jute Farley came in.

Randy scowled. Big business always had the dough to whitewash over the cracks that appeared in its sordid affairs.

Tying off his horse in front of the large building, he stepped up to the door and hustled into the entrance lobby without knocking. Such would be the expected arrival of a hard-assed gunnie.

The little man in reception was taken aback by his sudden appearance.

'Can I help you, sir?' blinked Ephraim Stokes from behind a pair of wire spectacles. Noting the dishevelled appearance of the newcomer, Stokes gave an imperious sniff of disdain. 'Do you have an appointment?'

The toady's supercilious manner immediately nettled the gunfighter. There was no need for play-acting. 'I wanna see the guy in charge,' he snapped gruffly.

'He is in a meeting and cannot be disturbed,' warbled the lackey.

Randy ignored the little man's response. 'And I wanna see him *now*!' The final word shot out like a bullet from a gun.

Striding purposefully over to a large oak door with the name of the said Jethro Tindale emblazoned in gothic script on a gilt-edged plaque, he made to enter the hallowed inner sanctum.

'You can't go in there,' howled the panic-stricken employee waving his hands around windmill fashion. 'Mr Tindale is a very busy man and cannot be disturbed.'

Randy swung on his heel, at the same time drawing his revolver and jabbing the lethal weapon at the hovering clerk.

'What's your name, tinhorn?' he rasped.

'Eph-phraim S-Stokes,' stuttered the ashen-faced clerk, his beady eyes gaping wide at the menacing pistol.

'Well then, Ephraim,' growled the intruder in a deeply cutting voice, 'I suggest you tell the boss he's got an extra appointment if'n you wanna stay healthy. You understand my meaning, fella?' The gun floated in front of Stokes's face like a mesmerizing rattlesnake.

'Y-yes, sir, immediately, s-sir,' grovelled the clerk, unable to remove his bulging orbs from the wagging pistol. Randy was enjoying himself. He hadn't had so much fun in a coon's age. 'Just take a seat, sir, and I will tell Mr Tindale you are here.'

Stokes moved to the door, knuckles raised to knock when a new thought occurred to him. 'Erm, who shall I say wishes to see him?'

'Just tell him that Jute sent for me.'

'Yes, sir. Jute sent for you.'

'That's right.' Randy speared the clerk with a malevolently evil eye. 'So get on with it.' He stamped his boot hard on the wooden floor. The little dude almost jumped out of his skin as he scuttled through the door.

In less than a minute, the clerk reappeared and tentatively gestured for Randy to enter the agency manager's office. It was a sumptuous room boasting all the trappings of success including the largest desk Randy had ever seen. Leather-bound books lined the walls, and a carpet thick enough to swallow a hog covered every spare inch of the floor.

Business was clearly booming for the Green River Development Agency. Randy briefly considered what need such a company had for driving out the homesteaders on the Dirty Devil.

He was not accorded any further time to speculate as Jethro Tindale emerged from behind his desk, arm outstretched in greeting. Dressed in a smart tailor-made suit and white frilly shirt, his oily smile was as bogus as the hairpiece that adorned his obviously bald dome.

'Welcome to Monticello, Mister. . . ?' Eyebrows raised, he waited for his ill-kempt visitor to supply the missing appendage.

'Mancos,' supplied the grim-faced gunfighter.

'Well Mr Mancos—'

'Just Mancos,' interrupted the visitor curtly. 'Jute Farley wired me in Rock Springs saying there's work down this way that pays well.' He paused to select a cigar from the humidor on the manager's desk. With infinite slowness, he lit up. Drifting curls of blue smoke eased from between pursed lips. All the while, the snake-eyes held the twitchy land agent with their hypnotic stare. 'Maybe you can point me in the right direction.'

'Mr Farley told me that he was expecting some new, erm . . . employees,' resumed the fidgety businessman.

Tindale was always nervous in the presence of men who lived, and quite often died, by the gun. But the company wanted this valley cleared, and there was no other way of ensuring that situation was accomplished within the time limit he had been given.

Tindale's head felt itchy beneath the hot peruke, although he dared not scratch it in the presence of this mean-eyed gunslinger. Instead, he paced up and down the room, attempting to maintain a boss-employee relationship. It was a struggle the land agent deemed he was in jeopardy of losing.

Randy could have continued to enjoy baiting the scheming tenderfoot, but he did not want to remain here any longer than was absolutely necessary. Securing the information he sought was the paramount issue.

'So where can I find Farley?' he said, letting the fish off the hook. 'Sooner me and my pard get started the better.'

Tindale was only too willing to supply the required directions. Anything to get this unsavoury character out of his hair – an unfortunate turn of phrase perhaps.

'The bailiffs are camped at Bullfrog Basin,' said Tindale, having regained his composure. 'It's a side valley off Glen Canyon.' Randy couldn't help smiling at the title given to Farley's gang of hardcases. 'Head south from here on the Blandings road for ten miles. Keep an eye open for the right fork. It's signposted so you can't miss the turn-off. The ferry crossing at Pike's Gulch will get you safely to the west bank of the Colorado. The entrance to the canyon is straight ahead.'

Randy nodded sagely. He was well acquainted with the territory. Although he did not want this slippery eel to know that.

'How long will it take to get there on horseback?'

'Leave here at daybreak and you ought to reach the basin by mid-afternoon,' supplied the eager land agent attempting to usher this dour gunman to the door. 'Now, if there is nothing else, I have a meeting to attend.'

Randy stood his ground. He wasn't finished yet.

'What about lookouts?' he asked. 'Me and Mr Wilks don't want to get ourselves shot up, now, do we?'

Tindale wrinkled his nose, an indication that such

a notion was immaterial to him. 'Mr Farley normally posts two on either side of the canyon,' he sniffed.

That was all Randy needed to know. So, after appropriating a couple more of the excellent Havanas from the desk, he allowed himself to be escorted to the door. And, with a smirking flourish, he departed uttering a final comment with regard to Jethro Tindale's supposedly discreet headgear.

'You'd be advised to acquire some better glue for that carpet on your head, Mr Tindale,' he smirked. The land agent blinked owlishly, his hand inadvertently straying to the said appendage, 'It's about to slip off.'

SEVEN

BULLFROG BASIN

It was mid morning when the two partners crossed the mighty Colorado by means of the ferry at Pike's Gulch. Instead of spending the night in the vicinity of Monticello as the land agent had expected, Randy had deemed it advisable that they put some distance between themselves and any possible source of danger.

'Why can't we stay in town overnight?' enquired Luke. 'Jim Daly who runs the livery stable often let me sleep over in a vacant stall.'

Randy pointed out that there was every possibility that some of the gang might visit the town. 'It's on the cards that Farley himself might arrive unannounced. He's bound to keep in regular contact with that slimy toad at the agency,' he remarked, as they followed a narrow trail behind some low knolls that effectively kept them hidden from any prying eyes. 'Neither of us wants that pesky hound dog eyeballing us afore we're good and ready.' Then another thought occurred to him. 'And just like Mancos and Wilks, there could be other road agents from my past on his payroll.'

Luke nodded. 'I see what you mean.'

Once they had crossed the river, Randy forked right off the trail into Bullfrog Basin in order to avoid being spotted by the ever-watchful eyes of the camp sentinels. Striking out through a plethora of loose boulders and cholla cactus, he picked a tortuous course over the rough terrain. His aim was to circle around behind the canyon where the Farley gang were ensconced making an approach up the more gently shelving rear escarpment.

Even so, it proved to be a nerve-shredding experience, the only access to the mesa being via a narrow exposed shelf of loose stones. This was not the place for careless manoeuvring. One slip of shod hoofs and they would be tipped over the edge of the cliff face. Extreme caution was the order of the day which meant that progress up the ever-steepening shelf was slowed to a that of a desert tortoise.

Emergence onto the flat topped mesa was sudden. All around, the landscape was stark and austere. Dessicated clumps of thorn and juniper struggled for survival amidst the bare rock of the plateau.

Dismounting, they left their mounts ground hitched and walked to the edge of the abrupt downfall a hundred yards distant.

Randy signalled for Luke to get down onto his stomach as they slithered snake-like up to the very edge of the precipice. Peering over the lip of the rock wall, Randy was pleased that his navigation had been spot on.

A smug grin creased the rugged features as Snake-eyes avidly scanned the encampment laid out some 500 feet below. It was extensive. Farley appeared to have appropriated an old pueblo settlement that had been abandoned. It afforded the ideal place to site a camp. Randy was forced to concede that his nemesis had chosen well.

The smile slipped from his face to be replaced by a disquieting frown.

This was not going to be anywhere near as simple a task as he had anticipated. The narrow canyon opening out into the broad amphitheatre known as Bullfrog Basin would be impossible to breach. A scattering of tents was interspersed with the more permanent pueblo dwellings. Behind, a sheer wall of solid rock reared up in a vertical cliff face which meant that any assault would have to be made head on.

Randy scratched his ear. A small number of well-placed defenders could hold off an army down there indefinitely.

And judging by the number of cooking fires, the outlaw was not short of personnel. He could see that they even had women, no doubt attending to the domestic chores, as well as satisfying the more earthy demands of Farley's crew. Snake-eyes probed every nook and crevice searching for any sign of Jan Bowdry, but without success. The gang leader must have secreted her away to service his own personal needs.

The odious conjecture stuck in Randy's throat. His fists clenched into tight balls, the knuckles blanching white as snow.

Much as his baser instincts cried out to dash in there with all guns blazing, the more prudent aspect of his character knew that a direct assault was out of the question. Taking out Jute Farley was going to require copious amounts of guile and cunning.

At least the skunk was now two recruits down. But there could easily be others on the way.

'When we gonna take them?' asked Luke, shouldering his rifle. He was more than eager to get started. Youthful exuberance fecklessly shrugged aside the harsh reality of the situation.

Randy laid a monitory hand on the rifle barrel.

'We ain't,' he asserted firmly.

Luke surveyed his partner with wide-eyed astonishment.

'What do you mean?'

'I mean, this needs thought and planning.'

'Why?' rapped the boy. 'Them dung beatles are holding Ma down there someplace. We gotta get her out.'

'Don't you think I know that, boy?' responded the older man vehemently. 'But there are too many of 'em. And they are well dug in. No way can the two of us hope to do anything effective. Except like as not get ourselves killed,' he stressed.

The look of contempt evident in his son's eyes bit deep into the gunfighter's soul.

'Never thought the great Snake-eyed Randy Cole

would give up without even firing a single shot.' The scornful indictment was delivered with venom.

'I ain't giving up, kid,' he responded with equal vehemence. 'But we need to gather some reinforcements together if we're to have any chance of winkling these critters out of their nest.'

'So who have you got in mind?'

Randy was given no opportunity to voice his reply.

The ominous sound of a revolver hammer ratcheting back broke into the caustic repartee.

Randy froze, his right hand automatically straying to the holstered six-shooter.

'Don't neither of you turkeys try anythin' clever if'n you wanna stay healthy.' The throaty tones of an avid whiskey drinker cut through the ozone. The speaker had not missed Randy's sly manoeuvre. 'Move another inch and I'll ventilate yer mangy carcasses with hot lead.'

Randy cursed under his breath. He should have been more careful. Underestimating the devious mind of a treacherous skunk like Jute Farley had been a grave error of judgement. One for which he and his new-found kin might well pay the ultimate penalty. If they emerged from this shindig in one piece, he vowed that no such disregard for his quarry's shrewdness would be repeated.

Farley certainly appeared to have all the angles covered.

'Now lift that hogleg nice and easy like,' ordered the gruff voice, 'and toss it behind you.' Then, to Luke, 'And the same for you with that Sharps, kid.

Any false moves and you're a gonner. Got that?'

Luke understood only too well.

Once both weapons had been disposed of, the gunman relaxed. 'OK, now turn over onto yer backs,' he ordered, 'and let's see what sort of critters feel the need to stick their pryin' beaks into our business. Jute's gonna be mighty anxious to find out what your game is.'

Once he'd had time to marshal his thoughts, Randy was confident of being able to extricate the two of them from what could have been a precarious situation. The poor sucker was playing right into his hands. It was just like tickling a trout. Randy felt like laughing out loud.

He had been in this position twice before. On the first occasion, it had been Clint Bowdry who had come to the rescue. Following that incident, Randy had taken out his own personal insurance policy. That same indemnity was about to be called upon to nullify another of Jute Farley's henchmen.

Randy's whole body tensed. Tight-lipped, breathing on hold, he slowly levered himself over onto his back. At the same time, and hidden from the gunman's view, he reached down and palmed the thin stiletto concealed in a boot sheath.

Then.

All it took was a single fluid movement and the deadly blade was winging towards its target.

The humbugged jasper never knew what struck him. One minute the two interlopers were completely at his mercy, the next he was gagging on his own blood. A crimson fountain pulsated from the severed artery where the glinting steel protruded from the unfortunate guy's neck.

Surprise and shocked bewilderment at the sudden change in fortunes was etched across the pox-ravaged kisser. This was not how it was meant to be.

His mouth opened. But only a choking gurgle emerged. The guy staggered back, then sank to his knees, collapsing like a rag doll, dead to the world.

A sudden gush of suppressed air hissed from between Randy's pursed lips as the pent-up tension eased.

Luke could only gape at the ambusher's twitching torso.

No greenhorn where sudden and violent death was concerned, Randy quickly recovered. He scrambled to his feet. Hustling over to the dead man, he extricated the knife and wiped it clean on the guy's shirt.

'I ain't never set eyes on this dude before,' he remarked, as if nothing untoward had occurred. 'Must be another hired gun brought in by Farley to help with his dirty work.' His next comment was addressed to Luke. 'Give me a hand to lug this body over to that ravine yonder.'

The boy remained frozen in shock.

'Come on, boy!' snapped the gunfighter impatiently. 'This ain't no time to get squeamish. We have to lose this guy. Make out he's upped sticks and scarpered. If Farley finds him, he'll know somebody's onto his game and send out trackers to hunt us down.' He toed the boy with a less than gentle prod to stimulate some form of animation. 'You hear me, boy?'

'Y-Yeah!' mumbled Luke struggling to his feet. 'I g-guess so.'

Avenging his father and rescuing his mother was becoming a far more brutalizing experience than the boy had ever considered. It was a chastening thought. But his stubborn streak did not allow for any wavering hesitancy. He had made a vow and would see it through to the bitter end no matter what that might be.

The corpse disappeared into the narrow crack. Five seconds later a dull splash informed Randy that the outlaw had hit an underground stream.

'Nobody will come aross that turkey this side of Judgement Day,' he announced with satisfaction. Having removed any evidence of their surreptitious spying, Randy knew they had to get out of Bullfrog Basin, and fast, There was no knowing when the guard would be missed.

Inside of an hour, the two riders had negotiated the hazardous descent back down to the foothills of Glen Canyon without mishap. Another hour and they had reached the broad swell of the Colorado.

Unfortunately, the winching cable attached to the ferry at Pike's Gulch had frayed. It was laid up, marooned on a rising tongue of land in mid-stream.

Randy was unable to control the torrent of lurid epithets that found his young partner's ear humming.

'Sorry about that,' Randy apologized, his tanned features assuming the russet grain of a Utah sunset. 'Couldn't help myself.'

The boy laughed. 'Pa was just the same when some'n niggled him like that. He sure got some stick from Ma though. She never could cotton to bad language.' For a brief instant, the grim scenario in which they were engaged faded from the forefront of his thoughts.

Randy was almost minded to voice his agreement. But that would have meant he was acquainted with Jan Bowdry. Complications of that nature he could do without having to explain under the present circumstances. Maybe later when all this had been settled, he would set the boy straight. Then again . . . Jan had laid her cards out on the table on that score.

He pushed the dilemma to the back of his mind.

With the ferry out of commission, they had no choice but to head south-west along the river-bank until another crossing point could be located.

Daylight was on the wane when a cluster of dwarf willow sprouting on either side of the river caught Randy's attention. When linked to the rippling texture of the silvery drift, he surmised that although more than a half-mile wide, the water was sufficiently shallow to enable a safe crossing to be made.

EIGHT

BOLT FROM THE BLUE

Jute Farley barged straight into the office of the Green River Development Agency. Tindale dropped his pen in surprise. He had been caught unawares. A savage growl of indignation hovered on his lips as an ugly ink blot splashed across the document he had been about to sign.

He somehow managed to contain himself on recognizing the intruder. None the less his lip curled with obvious distaste. He resented the outlaw's cocky manner and accorded the interloper a disdainful regard.

There was no love lost between the pair. But each was aware of the need to get along businesswise, albeit in a rather vacillating manner.

'Do you never think to knock before entering a room?' sneered the agent frostily. 'This is a private office. I could easily have been involved with a client.'

'Or been caught with yer pants down,' chuckled Farley gleefully. 'I know all about you and Belle Santee from the Chuckaluck.'

A rosy flush suffused the agent's smooth cheeks. He quickly hurried on. 'So what is it you want?' he snapped, trying to regain the higher ground.

'The boys have been askin' when the next sucker is gonna receive our unique removal service.' He reached over and extracted a cigar from the humidor on the agent's desk. Lighting up, he puffed appreciatively on the expensive Havana before continuing, 'They're gettin' a bit restless – wanna know when it's the big payday.'

'You know the answer to that,' chided Tindale. 'As soon as the valley's been cleared of settlers, you'll all get your money. There's only Brad Hogan and Milt Freeberg left. I'll let you know when to move in on them. But we need to take things slowly, otherwise the state legislature will become suspicious. And that would never do, would it?'

He laid a caustic eye on his tetchy accomplice, then lowered his voice a tone to emphasize the gravity of his next remark. 'And no more trouble. Burning out the Bowdry place was bad news. It could have brought the law down on our heads if'n I hadn't succeeded in greasing a few palms. Any more touches like that and you can say goodbye to the fat bonus you were promised.'

Farley snarled. His hand strayed to the pistol on his hip.

'Don't threaten me, fella,' he growled. 'I did you a favour there. Bowdry needed teachin' a lesson. Burning him out will make the other nesters toe the line.'

Tindale was struggling to maintain his cool.

Watching the dangerous gang boss insolently strutting around and enjoying one of his best cigars reminded the agent that too many visitors seemed to think they could wander into his office and call the shots. First that galoot Mancos and now Farley. But Jethro Tindale was no gunman and knew that Farley operated on a short fuse. He could not afford to antagonize the hardcase.

Instead he decided to change the subiect.

'Has Mancos and and his partner arrived yet?' he asked dabbing his face with a silk monogrammed handkerchief.

A frown darkened Farley's granite features, the black moustache twitching in vexatious accord.

'How did you know about those two?'

'Mancos called in here yesterday asking after directions to your camp,' replied Tindale. 'He said that you wired him in Rock Springs.'

Farley puffed hard on the cigar, his narrowed eyes staring at the wall. Something was wrong here. He paced the room trying to figure out what it was.

'They never arrived at Bullfrog Basin,' he muttered, shaking his head, the broad forehead wrinkled in concentration. His next comment was addressed to the land agent. 'And how come they knew to call on you for directions? I never mentioned that in the wire.'

Tindale replied with an unknowing shrug. 'Maybe Mancos just called in by chance.'

'I don't hold with coincidences,' Farley rapped impatiently.

Further deliberations on the issue were interrupted by a loud knock on the office door. It was followed immediately by another. Someone was in a panic.

'Come in!' shouted Tindale.

A heavy set jasper clearly in need of bathhouse treatment hustled into the office. Bill Tanner's dishevelled appearance pointed to a hard ride. He ignored the land agent as he gasped out his news directly to Farley.

'We've found Buffalo Jacks,' he blurted out, sucking in a great lungful of air.

An ugly grimace clouded Farley's visage. The gang leader squared his shoulders. 'So? The double-crossin' rat has been caught, has he?' The acrimonious query required no response and received none. 'I'll skin the bastard alive, then stake his mangy hide out fer the ants to feed on. Nobody quits the gang without my say so.'

'No, boss!' quaked Tanner, eyes wide with trepidation. Nobody liked to be the bearer of bad tidings. 'You got it wrong. Jacks was already dead when we found the body. It was splayed out on the rocks where Arrowmint Creek flows out the mesa bottom.' Tanner paused and imbibed another gulp of air before continuing, 'And that ain't all.'

'Go on!' snapped the nettled gang leader.

'Looks like he was stabbed and his body thrown into the ravine on Flatback Mesa where he was on guard.'

Silence bounced off the walls of the opulent surroundings.

Jute Farley was in a quandary.

Wilks and Mancos had failed to arrive. And now Buffalo Jacks had been killed. Could the two incidents be connected?

Farley turned to the land agent.

'What was this jigger like who called himself Mancos?'

Tindale considered. 'Tall and rangy with thick blond hair. He was no spring chicken, but still looked well able to handle himself.'

'Anythin' else?' pressed Farley. A sense of urgency made his voice sound panicky. 'An unusual feature maybe?'

Tindale's browed creased in thought.

'I did notice a scar on his left cheek. It was white in contrast to the rest of his face,' concluded the land agent.

The description was scant and lacking in substance. Yet it was somehow vaguely familiar to the outlaw boss.

One thing was for sure: it was most definitely not Mancos.

The two henchmen rode in silence.

Bill Tanner knew when to keep his big mouth

firmly shut. Normally a gregarious individual, it was a struggle for the outlaw not to question his leader's dour expression.

A frightened kangaroo rat scuttled across the trail causing Farley's cayuse to rear up on its hind legs. Yet even that failed to dent the gang leader's concentrated fixation on the distant crenellation of the Henry Mountains. But his thoughts were far removed from the impressive vista.

The identity of the mysterious stranger still itched at his craw.

Then it struck him.

That livid cheek scar was the all important clue. Like a slap in the face, a veritable bolt from the blue, the dreaded image of Snake-eyed Randy Cole swam before his bulging peepers.

The Judas had managed to evade the retribution he knew would be exacted when Cole was released from the pen. He had done that by settling down across the border in Canada.

But Farley had always been drawn to a life on the prod. So when he heard that jaspers of his ilk were in demand for 'land clearance' down in Utah, the temptation of returning to his old ways was irresistible.

Sweat beaded the gang-leader's brow as the realization dawned that Randy Cole was back. And the guy was on his case. His stomach lurched. The weathered face blanched visibly.

Sensing that Bill Tanner was aware of his tense manner, Farley shrugged off the despondency that had threatened to consume his thoughts. He needed to take control and rid himself of this thorn in his side. After all, Cole was only one man against Farley's gang of hired gunnies.

After leaving Tindale's office, he had asked around the saloons of Monticello if any strangers had been seen. Nothing untoward had been reported, but he could not afford to underestimate a turkey of Randy Cole's ilk.

The guy had run a successful operation for years without having his collar felt by the law. It was only Farley's betrayal that had led to his eventual capture and imprisonment. And he would settle for nothing short of Jute Farley's hide pinned to his saddle. Especially once he learned that Clint Bowdry had been shot and his wife abducted.

Farley turned to address his sidekick.

'Because that sap Tindale opened his big mouth, this guy knows that we're camped at Bullfrog Basin,' he propounded thoughtfully. 'And like as not it was him that did fer Buffalo Jacks.'

'What you plannin' to do then, boss?'

'We gotta nail the bastard. And quickly before he picks off any more of the boys.' Farley was more concerned for his own skin, but he couldn't let that fact be known. 'My guess is he'll need help now he knows I've put a sizeable gang together.'

Taut furrows creased Farley's face. Nervous fingers pulled at the black moustache. The notion that Snake-eyes was on his tail was enough to weaken the stoutest heart.

He surmised that his adversary would not want to

stick around Glen Canyon longer than necessary. Cole would also have realized by now that Wilks and Mancos failing to turn up would have alerted the gang. And with so many enemies hunting him down, the varmint would need a bolt hole.

But where would he go for help?

There were still members of the old gang out there who held a grudge against Jute Farley. They would want nothing more than to buy him a one-way ticket to Boot Hill. And the nearest as far as he could recall was Logan Hands. Last he heard the henpecked galoot was still living in Durango.

Farley snapped his fingers excitedly as the answer to his dilemma announced itself. Setting his black hat straight, a tight smile cracked the granite-hard exterior.

'I'm goin' back to the Basin,' he said with firm conviction. 'You wait at Pike's Gulch. I'll send two of the boys to join you. This dude's headed fer Durango. You can head him off by takin' the short cut through Blackstone Pass.' He fixed the burly tough with a baleful glare. 'And make darned sure he don't get there.'

Randy Cole tugged his hat down to shade out the rising sun. He and Luke had set off from their overnight camp before dawn. Yet by mid-morning the sun was hot enough to melt the eyes of a gopher. Heads drooping low, a yellow sheen of dust settled over their sweating faces.

The pace was relentless. Too much time had

already been wasted on account of the stricken ferry at Pike's Gulch. And it was vital that they reach Durango soon if Jan Bowdry was to be safely rescued. There was no telling how a scumball like Jute Farley would react once he figured out the truth. And Randy was under no illusions that the treacherous dog would arrive at the right conclusions.

And sooner rather than later.

Hunkered out of sight behind a cluster of rocks overlooking the approach to Blackstone Pass, the three bushwhackers settled down to await their victims. Bill Tanner shielded his eyes against the sun's harsh glare as he scanned the twisting trail meandering up a boulder-strewn grade from the plains below.

All travellers heading for the Colorado state line would have to pass this way. And the outlaw was confident their quarry would not have reached the pass before them.

Arby Sinclair who operated the Pike's Gulch ferry had assured the three men that a jasper answering to the description supplied by Jute Farley had headed downriver the previous afternoon.

'Took me the rest of the day to fix that cable,' he grumbled while scratching his ample belly. 'Had to work all through the goddamned night.'

But Tanner and his two sidekicks exhibited no interest in the woes of the whining ferryman. All they needed was for Sinclair to divulge where the killer of Buffalo Jacks had crossed the Colorado. Jacks had been a well liked member of the Farley gang, and the three trail birds were intent on avenging his untimely demise.

'D'yuh reckon he'll reach Blackstone Pass afore us?' pressed a thin whipcord dude by the name of Fingers McCoy. Of indeterminate age and sporting a neatly trimmed goatee, McCoy had earned the unusual moniker on account of his right hand boasting an extra digit. The offending appendage protruded from between thumb and forefinger like a dead twig. To survive the inevitable taunts, he had been forced early on in his owlhoot career to make the switch to a left-handed draw.

This mandatory requirement was now displayed to full effect.

'You'd be wise to answer the man, Arby,' advised the third gunman as McCoy's revolver prodded the reluctant ferryman's ample midriff menacingly. 'Fingers ain't known for his patience.'

Just like barbers and bartenders, ferrymen had big ears. In similar fashion, they only passed on their acquired fund of extensive knowledge when the right price was paid. Or when some rooster threatened to ventilate their hides. Fingers McCoy looked as if he would have no compunction in carrying out the latter.

Sinclair quickly determined that money was not about to change hands on this occasion and that his continued good health was at stake, not to mention the fact that he had to deal with these jiggers on a day-by-day basis.

The hooded black eyes behind the Smith &

Wesson obviated any negotiation.

'I t-told 'em to c-cross at Horsetail Bend where the river is shallow,' stammered the nervous ferryman. 'That's around twenty miles to the south-west.'

'How far to Blackstone Pass?' rapped Tanner.

'No more'n a half day's ride with fresh mounts,' replied Sinclair, adding as an afterthought, 'you should easily get there afore them.'

Squint Regan lifted a quizzical eyebrow.

'You mean this guy had a partner?' he suggested.

'If'n you can rate the Bowdry kid as a partner,' smirked Sinclair.

'You mean Clint Bowdry's younker?' came from a decidedly puzzled Bill Tanner.

'One and the same.'

'What in tarnation is this galoot doin' with a kid in tow?' queried Regan.

'Don't matter none to us,' added Tanner.

'And draggin' a kid along is bound to slow him down,' interjected McCoy. 'We can take 'em both out at Blackstone Pass.'

'Easy as fallin' off a log,' laughed Regan.

'OK boys, let's hit the trail,' declared Tanner, who had appointed himself unofficial leader of this venture. 'We got us some fish to fry.'

'Jute's gonna be mighty pleased when we catch us two birds for the price of one,' announced Squint Regan breezily while scurrying across to his cayuse.

'Ought to merit a bonus. What d'yuh reckon, Bill?'

McCoy's proposal received a shrugged response.

'Maybe. Let's just get the job done first.'

The ferryman mopped his sweating brow while heaving a sigh of relief as the trio of hardcases disappeared in a cloud of yellow dust.

Next stop Blackstone Pass.

NINE

BUSHWHACKED

'Get that blamed rifle down!' hollered Bill Tanner. 'D'yuh want to give them turkeys an advance warnin' of our presence up here?'

McCoy snarled into his beard. His hand dropped to the butt of his revolver.

'Easy there, Fingers,' cautioned Squint Regan. 'Bill's just bein' careful. Nothin' wrong in that, is there?'

McCoy was the fastest gunhand in the gang. But he retained the good sense to understand that Tanner was right and was acting under orders from Jute Farley. And that was one ice-cold critter you didn't mess with.

The long barrel of the Winchester was quickly lowered.

But it was too late.

A half-mile below the lip of the pass, Randy Cole drew his mount to a halt and urgently nudged both horses into the cover of a large boulder. Snake-eyes had been well named. Constant appraisal of the surrounding terrain through which they passed had now paid dividends.

'Why have we stopped?' enquired a perspiring Luke Bowdry.

Randy pointed to the heights above.

'We got company.'

The announcement was blunt and emphatic.

'How d'yuh figure that?' asked the sceptical boy squinting in the direction of the prodding digit. 'I can't see anything.'

'The glint of sun on metal,' clarified the gunfighter narrowing his probing gaze. At that instant a flight of jays fluttered skywards, squawking and complaining at some disturbance from the direction of the pass. 'And that proves it,' he iterated. 'There's bushwhackers up there just waiting to pick us off like bottles on a wall.'

Without further ado, he dismounted, dragging the Henry from its saddle boot. Luke joined him with his trusty Sharps.

'The bastard's gone and spotted us,' rasped an irate Bill Tanner. 'It was that blamed rifle of yourn.' He shot McCoy a baleful glare.

'No way!' protested the outlaw. 'It was you disturbin' them jays.'

'Cut the snipin', you guys,' interrupted Regan with some measure of vexation. 'No point arguin' over spilt milk. What's done is done. The question is how do we play it from here?'

That notion evoked a tense silence that matched the grim frowns now clouding the bushwhackers' worried faces.

Once again, Tanner took charge.

'Them turkeys are goin' nowhere,' he asserted. 'They're stuck down there. All we have to do is wait 'em out.'

Peering from behind a boulder, Regan's squinting peepers noted a brown slouch hat poking out like a sore thumb above the pale ochre rocky terrain below. A morbid smile split the outlaw's ribbed features. Taking careful aim, he let fly with a couple of shots from his rifle.

The hat flew up into the air.

'Got me one.'

The outlaw's response was a raucuous whoop of triumph.

'Good shootin', Squint,' concurred Tanner.

'We still gotta take out the other jasper,' said McCoy. 'And he'll be on his guard now. We could be stuck here for hours.'

'You're right there, Fingers,' agreed a chastened Tanner. He considered for a moment. 'You're the best shot at close quarters. Circle round to the right and try and get in behind. We'll keep him pinned down from up here.'

What the three bushwhackers did not realize was that they themselves were being hoodwinked.

Perceiving that they could indeed be trapped here indefinitely by an unknown enemy, Randy intended playing the critters at their own game. He instructed

Luke to keep up a steady fire from his concealed position thus making the ambushers think they had the survivor bang to rights.

Falling back on the old hat trick had been an afterthought – one that he never figured seasoned gun hands would fall for. The exhilarating cheer filtering down from the rocks above had proved the theory that the old chestnuts were often the best.

And he had correctly surmised the bushwhackers' assumption that having only one victim to deal with would tip their hands. They would now want to finish off the job quickly.

Randy crawled over to an overhanging cliff with a rock shelf halfway up where he could watch for any surreptitious assault from above. He did not have long to wait.

A scratching of boots on loose gravel informed him that somebody was approaching down a gully. Randy cautiously peered out from his hidden perch. The guy had drawn his revolver. A thin smile was pasted to the gaunt façade as the killer moved in behind the line of fire expecting an easy kill.

Randy waited, muscles tense, nerves drawn tighter than a whore's corset.

Fingers McCoy suspected nothing as he picked his way below the overhanging shelf of rock. When he was directly beneath the ledge, Randy silently dropped down behind him. It all happened in the blink of an eye. His left arm brusquely encircled the gunman's neck in a throttling embrace. At the same time, the lethal blade of his stiletto was driven hard into the jigger's back with ruthless efficiency.

McCoy never knew a thing about it as the whispering sigh of expelled air hissed from the dead outlaw's open mouth. At least it was a quick end. And a silent one, which was how Randy had planned it.

Even Luke was unaware that one of their adversaries had been neutralized.

Shaking off the inevitable shock to the system that such a brutal slaying can impose on the perpetrator, Randy scuttled up the gully down which McCoy had so recently descended. Keeping his head well below the skyline, he soon reached the crest of Blackstone Pass.

Regan and Tanner were pumping shells down towards their supposed quarry below. The first thing they knew that things had not gone McCoy's way was a harsh order from their rear.

'Drop them smokepoles and raise your hands!'

The two froze.

'Throw them guns away now!' snapped Randy acidly. 'Else I'll blast your poxy hides straight into the hereafter.' The icy tone was intended to instil fear and instant obedience.

But Tanner was not so easily intimidated. He uttered a manic snarl of defiance.

'No way, you son of a bitch!'

Pivoting on his left heel, the gunman swivelled and let rip with the Winchester. But Randy had already anticipated such a manoevre. The bullets whistled over his head as he lay on his belly and pumped three slugs into the startled outlaw. Tanner reeled back pitching over the craggy lip into the empty void. A blood-curdling howl was cut short as the dead body thudded onto the rocks below the pass.

Randy's pistol immediately swung towards the third man. His snake-eyed gaze, flintlike and malevolent, held the cowering man in a grip of terror.

Squint Regan was no hero. He had seen enough. His rifle clattered on the stony ground, arms reaching skvwards.

'Don't shoot, mister.' he pleaded. 'I surrender. I'll tell you anything you want to know.'

Bloodlust had claimed Randy's soul. His gunhand tensed, trigger finger blanching white. Be was all for blasting the varmint. Just in time the red mist dissolved. It was the outlaw's desire to spill the beans that tipped the scales. Randy breathed out heavily. He had no desire to exact revenge in cold blood. That was the coward's way out.

Over the next ten minutes he questioned Regan on a number of issues concerning Jute Farley's intentions. His main concern was for the safety of Jan Bowdry.

'Farley has her locked up in an isolated but on the far side of the basin,' exclaimed Regan, who was only too eager to help. 'He only lets her out under the supervision of two guards. And then it's for no more than a brief spell.'

'Is she being treated OK?' Randy enquired.

'As well as can be expected,' replied the cringing outlaw. 'Jute's hopin' she'll come to accept him as her man eventually. But she's one sassy dame. That's what he likes about her.'

'Has he. . . ?' Randy hesitated to ask, although he had to know. 'Has he . . . you know?'

Regan knew exactly what he meant and had no intention of jeopardizing his continued good health.

'Not that I know of,' he stressed. 'Jute wants her to be . . . willing.'

Randy nodded, unsure whether to believe him. If it was true, he also knew that Farley would only wait so long before taking what he judged was his by right of conquest. Spoils for the victor. And if Jan continued to thwart his demands, the gang boss would not hesitate to get rid of her permanently.

The thought caused a twisted grimace to replace the worried frown of seconds before.

Squint Regan had likewise perceived the angry reaction.

'I swear, mister, none of the boys had anything to do with the lady's kidnappin'.' The tremor in Regan's contention testified to the outlaw's desperate need to distance himself from the gang-leader's actions. 'We're just paid hands doin' a job of work.'

Randy was not listening.

His final request for information concerned the layout of the outlaw hideaway. In particular, he was keen to learn of any back doors that could allow him an easy way in without being spotted. Especially those that were not guarded.

Down below the pass, Luke emerged from cover.

Witnessing Bill Tanner topple over the edge of the cliff face informed the boy that his partner had got the better of the bushwhackers.

'You ain't gonna shoot me are yuh, mister?' repeated Regan, his poor eye squinting like there was no tomorrow. It was an eventuality that now seemed distinctly feasible. 'I'll skip the territory. You won't see me agin, I promise.'

'I say we gun the bastard down just like he done my pa.'

Both men turned.

Luke Bowdry had his rifle pointed unerringly at the outlaw. He thumbed back the hammer. Regan was sweating buckets. His mouth flapped like a landed catfish but no sound emerged.

For a brief instant, Randy was stunned into immobility by the boy's vehement threat.

'Put the gun up, Luke,' he said quietly, so as not to spook the boy into some reaction he might later live to regret. 'There's been enough killing for one day.'

'This varmint deserves to join the others,' the boy accented, taking a step foward. 'Ain't that what the Bible teaches? An eye for an eye?'

'Not the one I heed!' Randy then stepped into the line of fire. 'I said there'll be no more killing.'

His even gaze willed the boy to lower his rifle.

Eventually the older man's fervent resolve paid off. He turned back to address a decidedly nervous Squint Regan.

'If I ever see you again, fella, you're buzzard bait,' he snarled. 'Now git!'

'S-sure, mister,' stuttered the relieved outlaw. 'And thanks.'

He hurried across to his horse, leapt into the saddle and dug his spurs in hard. The startled animal reared up almost unseating its rider. Regan frantically wrestled the cayuse back under control. One final glance at the good Samaritan and his feisty partner, then he galloped off into the setting sun.

'You should have let me gun him down,' ranted a still jittery Luke Bowdry once the outlaw had disappeared from view.

Randy knew that he had to rein in the boy's desire for unbridled revenge. He was acquiring a taste for killing. And watching him head down that trail made the gunfighter's blood run cold.

'You should only ever resort to terminal gunplay as a last resort,' he urged, resting his hands on the boy's trembling shoulders. 'And only when other methods have failed. I've seen too many young bucks think the answer to every problem is a fast draw and hot lead.' He held the youngster with a pleading look of understanding. 'You cotton to what I'm saying, boy?'

Luke nodded slowly, as the tension eased from his rigid frame.

'I guess so,' he murmured lowering the rifle. 'But that don't mean I aim to turn the other cheek.'

Randy's face cracked in a relaxed smile.

'You do and I'll slap it.'

TEN

SHAKEDOWN

They reached the Colorado mining town of Durango in three days.

Wagons, horses and pedestrians filled the busy street. The town was clearly benefiting from the prodigious yield of silver ore.

Randy prayed that his old sidekick was still in residence. He needn't have worried. Halfway down the wide main drag, a large sign jutted out from a two-storey emporium bearing the colourful appendage that read LOGAN AND MARTHA HANDS – PURVEYORS OF EVERYTHING. YOU WANT IT, WE'VE GOT IT!

To be sure an ambitious declaration.

It appeared that his old trail buddy had risen in Durango society since retiring from the owlhoot life. It now appeared that he owned the general store in which he had once been employed as a mere clerk. Martha Hands would be well pleased at her elevated status.

The gunfighter signalled their destination to his partner.

Both riders were caked in trail dust and badly in need of a bath. But first they needed to ascertain if Logan Hands would be willing to join them on the vengeance trail. Randy was only too aware of Martha's iron grip on her husband's every move.

Dismounting, they tied their horses to the hitching post and stepped up onto the boardwalk. Randy peered through the store window. There was no sign of either of the proprietors. All he could ascertain at first glance was a young assistant behind the counter. A man was being served with what appeared to be mining gear.

After the prospector had left, the two partners entered the store.

'A fine day is not, sir?' beamed the clerk with due deference. 'And I hear that the price of silver has gone up again.'

From their unkempt appearance, the guy had mistaken them for miners.

Randy ignored the pleasantries, preferring to get straight to the hub of the matter.

'Is Mr Hands available?' he asked tersely.

The clerk's manner assumed a more lofty bearing when his small talk was so curtly brushed aside.

'Can I enquire as to the nature of your business?' he crowed.

'Just tell Shake that it's in connection with the National Bank at Gunnison,' growled Randy deliberately laying on the hard-man image with a heavy hand.

He could barely maintain a straight face as the anxious clerk hustled into a room at the back of the store.

Logan Hands and his wife were having their luncheon.

'What is it, Colby?' he rapped impatiently. Hands was not well pleased at having his meal interrupted.

'There's a gentleman out front wanting to see you,' said the clerk.

'What does he want?'

The clerk frowned, a bemused expression warping his thin face.

'Something about the Gunnison Bank.' Colby Fudge shrugged. 'He said you'd know what he meant. He also called you. . . .' The clerk gulped before continuing.

'Well?' exclaimed Hands. 'Out with it, boy.'

'He referred to you, sir, as . . . Shake.'

The blood drained from the store-owner's face.

'What is this all about, Logan?' huffed his wife. 'You look as if you've seen a ghost. And what's all this about Gunnison?'

The only people who knew him as Shake Hands harked back to his days on the prod. He hadn't been called that moniker since the old gang had broken up. And that was back in '73.

Beads of sweat bubbled up on his forehead. So who could this dude be. Had the law finally tracked him down?

'What does he look like?' Hands asked, dabbing his brow with a handkerchief.

'I mistook him for a miner,' replied Fudge. 'And

he's got a boy in tow.'

'Do you know this man, Logan?' asked Martha Hands.

Her husband lifted his hands in ignorance.

This was getting more bizarre by the minute. But at least it didn't appear as if the guy was a lawman.

Hands stood up, straightened his necktie, and squared his shoulders. He was a big man. The intervening years had witnessed a distinct expansion of his waistline. But beneath the store-bought suit, Shake Hands still carried himself with a supple grace. He had lost none of his strength, muscle rather than flab filling out the expensive cloth.

Shrugging off the ribs of worry that threatened to contort his normally benign façade, Logan went out to meet the mysterious visitors. He pasted a glib smile onto his face.

'You wish to have words with me about some past issue, I believe,' he said, addressing the tall stranger who looked somehow familiar. His features were in shadow, concealed beneath a wide-brimmed slouch hat. 'Are we acquainted, sir?' he added with a puzzled frown.

Slowly and with purposeful deliberation, Randy removed the hat. A quirky grin spread across his handsome features. Even when covered by a clinging layer of trail dust, the tell-tale white cheek scar stood out proud and dominant.

Shake's mouth dropped open in amazement as recognition dawned.

'Randy!' he exclaimed. 'Snake-eyed Randy Cole!'

He grabbed his old boss's hand and shook it with heart-warming sincerity.

'It must be all of ten years.'

'Thirteen years ten months and twelve days to be exact.' The reply prickled with a hard-edged bite. 'That's what the pen does. Makes you appreciate what time you have left.'

'I feel bad about that, Randy,' sighed Hands. 'But when you never turned up at Frenchman's Creek, we assumed the worst. And decided to break up the gang and go our separate ways.' A steely glint replaced the warm glow. 'If'n I'd gotten my hands on that skunk, Jute Farley. . . .'

'No need to aplogize, Shake,' interjected Randy, reverting to his easy-going lilt. 'In fact, it's about Farley that I'm here.' He paused to emphasize his next remark. 'He's turned up in Utah.'

'You don't say.'

'And this young shaver is Clint Bowdry's boy. Or was!'

'You don't mean. . . .'

'It's a long story.'

'Then let's you and me mosey on down to the Saddle Tramp and have us a parley over some cold beers.'

'Suits me fine,' grinned Randy.

Hands turned and dug his large mitt into a candy jar.

'This should keep you busy until me and this old goat return,' enthused Hands. 'Do you like jigsaw puzzles?'

'Sure do,' shot back the boy eagerly.

'Well, my assistant here makes them with his very own jigsaw. Paints the picture on plywood, then cuts them out.' Hands winked at his assistant. 'He'll show you how its done, won't you, Colby?'

'Be my pleasure, Mr Hands.'

'And, Colby?'

'Yes, sir?'

'No mention to anyone about my visitor. You hear, boy?' He slung a thumb towards the back room where his wife was finishing her meal.

'My lips are sealed,' replied the young man seriously.

The two old buddies then left the store heading across the street to avail themselves of the refreshment afforded by the Saddle Tramp Saloon.

When they were seated in a booth at the rear of the saloon where no flapping ears could listen in to their confab, Shake's casual manner quickly assumed a more sombre outlook.

'So what's this all about, Randy?'

The ex-gang leader sucked in a deep breath.

For the next hour he appraised his old confederate of the intervening years since the betrayal at Deadman's Gulch. The stand-off in the cabin, his brutal incarceration in the state penitentiary, the search for Jute Farley, his new career in the production of that cowboy staple – fatback bacon. This latter brought the first hint of smile to the storekeeper's face.

There followed a narration of more recent

happenings that involved the sudden and unexpected appearance of the fly in the ointment, namely Jute Farley. Shake was especially angered by the death of Clint Bowdry at the hands of the Judas.

The only thing Randy deliberately withheld was the fact that Luke Bowdry was his son. All the gang were aware of his relationship with the boy's mother. But to reveal the paternal link would have released too many questions that he was not ready, nor willing, to answer.

Following the revelations, both men sat in silence. Shake Hands had much to contemplate. Not least the plans that Randy had outlined for the rescue of Jan Bowdry and the confrontation with Jute Farley.

After five minutes, Randy pressed Hands as to whether he would join him.

'So, are you in?'

Hands hesitated. Randy's heart sank.

At that moment, Martha Hands bustled into the saloon and made a bee-line for the two *compadres*.

'So here you are, Logan Hands,' she sniped, her voice strident and grating. 'The monthly accounts are still sitting on the parlour table. And you promised to clean out the ablutions tank today.' She sniffed imperiously on recognizing her husband's old buddy. 'And I see you've been at the drink as well.'

'Hello, Martha,' said Randy affecting a forced bonhomie. He raised his glass. 'Nice to see you again too after all these years.'

Martha Hands ignored the greeting. She had

always held her husband's old associates in the deepest contempt. And even after all this time, nothing appeared to have changed.

She was only a small woman, but effectively made up for her lack of inches with a belligerent and contentious manner. Round staring eyes peered from behind a pair of wire pince-nez giving her the appearance of a haughty dormouse. Randy struggled to understand how a man like Logan Hands could have become involved with such a starchy female.

Shake remained silent; he was clearly still very much under the thumb.

'Well?' piped up the harsh voice. 'What have you to say for yourself?'

Tight-tipped and flushed from an excess of the hard stuff, it was now Shake's turn to gird up his loins. Lurching to his feet, chair crashing over backwards, the big man towered over his diminutive wife. They had often been likened to a musical hall double act. But there was no humour in the big man's eyes now.

'Do the goddamned accounts yerself, woman!' he rasped. 'And you can get all your stuck-up cronies on the Temperance Committee to do your dirty work. I'm finished with it all.' He removed the apron he had forgotten about and threw it on the table. Then stumped off followed by a startled Randy Cole.

Martha Hands was too stunned to object.

Such a display of discord from her husband was beyond comprehension.

'I take it we're in business?' asked a tentative Randy Cole, who was still rather bemused by the sudden change in his old buddy.

'You're darned tootin' we are.'

Within a half-hour, the three riders were heading out of Durango following the left bank of the Animas River north to Silverton.

It was some time before Logan Hands felt sufficiently calmed to venture a response to Randy's unspoken puzzlement.

'I shoulda done that years ago,' he declared. A lazy smile cracked the taciturn demeanour. 'How I've stuck with that woman I'll never know.'

'Me neither,' agreed Randy.

Luke remained tight-lipped, suitably awestruck by their new partner.

The strange trio soon left Durango behind as they headed north to Silverton. It was the last place the ex-storekeeper had heard tell that Stripes Gifford was living.

The journey took them through deep gorges cloaked in dense stands of pine and aspen. Having arrived in the silver-mining boom town, a few casual enquiries brought them to a single cabin stuck on the edge of a shelf above the valley floor.

Here it was that Stripes Gifford had bought into what he had been assured was a rich vein of paydirt. Although one look at the crumbling home of their old associate was enough to indicate that the claim had been a bogus investment. But Gifford was nothing if not tenacious, insisting to all and sundry that a rich strike was imminent. After ten years of hard graft, it had still to arrive.

A small mousy individual with wisps of thinning grey hair poking from beneath his hat, he was delighted to meet up with his old buddies. And once Randy had filled him in on all the facts of their venture, Gifford was eager to participate.

'Glad you can join the party, Stripes,' breezed the gang leader. 'You still a dead shot with that Spencer?'

'As ever,' preened the miner, tipping a jug of moonshine to his lips. 'I can still peck out the eyes of a hawk at two hundred paces.'

'Let me have a look at that long gun, Stripes,' said Randy.

'Sure thing.' He handed the jug to Hands, then stood and moved over to the far side of the cabin.

As he did so, he tripped over Luke Bowdry's splayed-out legs and tumbled to the ground.

'Watch out there, fella,' said Hands helping the little guy to his feet.

'Not lookin' where I was a-goin',' he clucked, laughing off the error.

But Randy was not so sure. Nobody could have missed spotting the boy's long legs. He threw a frowning glance at Shake Hands.

Could it be that Stripes Gifford was going blind? Secure in his own cabin, the old outlaw would know exactly where everything was kept. But the unexpected had caught him napping.

There was only one way to determine the truth.

'Let's go outside,' suggested Randy, 'and have us

some shooting practice.'

Clutching the Spencer, Gifford stood on the edge of the rocky shelf and pointed to a tin can stuck on a tree stump some hundred yards distant.

'Watch this,' he said. After slipping a cartridge into the breech, he flipped back the hammer. Taking careful aim, he squeezed the trigger. The can shot up into the air.

Gifford yelped with delight. 'What about that then?'

'Great shot, Stripes,' praised Randy. 'Now let's see if'n you can hit that old buzzard squatting on the rock over yonder.'

Gifford screwed up his eyes.

'Just point me in the right direction, boys,' he said, trying not to exhibit any qualms.

'Over to your left by the large aspen.' Randy's words came out flat and lacklustre. Seeing his old friend vaguely attempting to achieve the impossible brought tears to his eyes.

'You can't see it, can you?' he stated blankly.

'Sure I can, he's over there.' Gifford swung his arm taking in the whole of the valley.

But he knew the game was well and truly up. The old guy's head drooped. Bashfully, he produced a pair of spectacles and slipped them on.

'How long you been like this?' enquired a concerned Logan Hands. The two had been close buddies in the old days.

Gifford shrugged.

'Bin gettin' worse over the past six months,' he

muttered. 'The specs help with close stuff like readin', but long distance is all a blur.' His glassy eyes focused on Randy. 'You give that backstabbin' Judas a bullet from me when you catch him, yuh hear, boss?'

'I sure will, Stripes.'

'If'n you're after gettin' the old gang back together, forget about Maverick.'

'Why?'

Before replying, Gifford ambled across to the cabin. After his recent ordeal he needed a drink. A hefty slug of the powerful elixir softened his gnarled features into a wistful expression.

'After the gang split, the two of us decided to strike out on our own. We headed south into New Mexico hoping to rob us a few stagecoaches. We figured that two of us would be enough.' He blinked at the sudden recollection. A coyote howled in the distance in sympathy. 'And we did all right, for a while. Then Maverick started gettin' careless. He paid the ultimate price.'

'What happened, Mr Gifford?' Luke was spellbound by this talk of hold-ups and gunplay from desperadoes who had lived outside the law.

'Well, son,' purred the old reprobate, pleased that he had an eager listener for his wayward tales. 'Maverick failed to maintain his hardware. He became lazy. And when you're on the owlhoot trail, the last thing a fella wants is fer his gun to jam.'

'Yeh! Don't I know it,' clamoured the excited boy.

'Same thing happened to me on the Green River.'

'Well, I hope yuh learned a valuable lesson, boy,' urged the old-timer.

'Sure did.'

'It was too late for Maverick. A driver let rip with both barrels of a Loomis. Blew him right out of the saddle.' Gifford's voice faltered as the image of his dead partner floated across his mind's eye. 'I lit out damn fast, and kept on ridin' until I quit the territory. That's when I came up here. Figured to try my hand at prospectin'. Ain't had much luck so far.' A gleam lit up his heavily lined face. 'But I live in hope. That's all a fella can do.'

Then he lapsed into silence.

'Don't suppose you know the whereabouts of Concho?' quizzed a doubtful Randy Cole.

Gifford scratched his greasy head.

'Fella came through here only last week. He said there was some guy in the pokey over at Telluride that could well have been the kid.' Even though Concho Sterling was now well into his thirties, Gifford still thought of him as a feisty young tearaway. 'When I questioned him further, it appeared that this guy wore silver conchos in a black hat.'

'This jigger say what he'd done?' posed Shake Hands leaning forward.

'Some'n about shootin' his way out of a gal's boudoir.' A throaty cackle erupted from the old boy's mouth. 'Seems like it was the mayor's wife he'd been a-dallyin' with.'

'Mighta guessed,' smirked Hands, helping himself

to the jug of moonshine.

'The guy never learns,' agreed Randy.

After some measure of speculative deliberation aided by liberal helpings of Stripes Gifford's excellent home-brewed hooch, he promulgated, 'Now all we gotta do is figure out a way of getting him out of the hoosegow.'

ELEVEN

TELLURIDE

The trail from Silverton pursued a tortuous route threading its way through the mountain fastness. Climbing gradually up over Lizard Head Pass, towering crags and fractured pillars of rock hemmed them in on all sides. Progress was slow. All too frequently the indistinct trail narrowed to little more than a deer run, occasionally petering out altogether.

Only by keeping the lofty upsurge of Red Mountain on their right hand was Randy sure that they were heading in the right direction. At this height, the heat of the summer sun had little effect and they were obliged to don sheepskin jackets to combat the penetrating wind that funnelled down the steep ravines. It was with a sigh of relief that on the morning of the third day, a cluster of buildings appeared in the valley far below.

This had to be Telluride.

It took the rest of the day to descend the meandering trail. Increasingly as height was lost, they came across groups of placer miners scrabbling in creek beds for elusive gold nuggets. Enquiries confirmed that they were indeed heading in the right direction.

'To Hell you ride, mister,' chortled one bearded wit. 'Only desperate men and the Devil come here. Which are you?'

Randy circumvented the light-hearted banter by gently quizzing the miner about more pressing matters.

'I heard tell there's a mean-eyed law officer down in Telluride.'

'That'll be Shad Baron.' The miner shook his head grimacing as he added, 'You'd be advised to watch yer step where that jigger's concerned. One false move and he'll have you locked up afore you can blink an eye.' The old sourdough snapped his fingers to emphasize the point. 'You fellas hopin' to stake a claim?'

Randy deftly sidetracked the verbose miner's enquiry.

'This turkey get much call to lean on his badge?' he asked casually, not wishing to appear over-inquisitive.

The other two riders bent over their saddlehorns, ears atuned to the miner's response.

'You betcha!' he cackled again. 'Baron locked a fella up only last week. Snazzy-lookin' dude too.' The old-timer lowered his voice, gesturing for them to move in closer. A pointless action as there was nobody in sight, the implication being that his next remark was of the sensitive variety. 'Appears as if he'd been caught with his pants down.' He accorded the two men a foxy wink. 'Get my drift, boys?'

Randy and his sidekick responded with dutiful nods.

'He shot the town mayor and tried to escape through the bedroom window. Trouble was the poor sap slipped and knocked hisself out. Didn't stand a chance of escapin' after that. The sheriff was there in a jiffy. He had to get a couple of the boys to carry this dude over to the jailhouse.' The chatty miner then twisted his wrinkled face in a petulant sniff. 'The mayor weren't no saint. I seen him sneakin' upstairs at the cathouse with a girl on each arm on more'n one occasion.'

But Randy had heard enough.

As soon as he could get in a word, Randy bade the lonely miner farewell. Little was said as the thoughtful trio of riders made their way down through the stands of thick pine to the flat valley floor.

It was Luke who voiced the hundred-dollar question.

'So how we gonna free this guy?'

Nobody voiced an opinion. That was something they would need to work out.

Entering the outer precinct of the town, it was immediately apparent where the wealthy citizens resided. Smart houses had been erected along a tree-lined boulevard. A stark contrast to the bustling mêlée that thronged the main street further along. Randy cracked a half smile at the notion of Concho attempting a rapid exit from one of the upstairs windows with his pants flapping about his legs.

The sheriff's office was halfway down on the left. It was the only brick-built structure in town located adjoining a gunshop. On the other side was a dress-maker's emporium. And unusually for a mining town, there were manequins in the window sporting the latest female apparel. A testament to this having become a more permanent settlement.

Randy's face tightened. If that were the case, maybe the law was likewise more efficient.

They would soon find out.

Dismounting, the three riders tied up at the hitching rail and stepped up onto the boardwalk.

Luke squared his young shoulders. Settling his gunbelt at an easy angle, he attempted to manoeuvre his face into a suitably tough expression in keeping with the hard-boiled surroundings.

It was Randy who broke into the boy's fanciful reveries.

'Keep your eye on the horses while Shake and me check out if our old buddy is the jasper locked up in here.' He slung a thumb at the solid oak door.

Luke scowled. A mean-eyed gunslinger didn't watch the horses. That was a wrangler's job.

'Do I have to?' grumbled the youngster, scowling.

Randy immediately picked up on his son's truculent manner. One thing he didn't need was having to wet-nurse the kid. These were dangerous waters with no room for arguing the toss once a course of action had been determined.

He speared the boy with the infamous snake-eyed regard, his forefinger jabbing to underscore the blunt remark that followed.

'Now you listen up, boy!' he rapped out. 'Anyone hitting the trail with Randy Cole takes orders. No whingers ride with me. I ain't got the time nor the patience for mealy-mouthed belly-aching.' There was a pause to let the import of his words register. 'You understand me? 'Cos if'n you don't, this is the end of the line. You go back to Monticello and wait on my return once this business is settled.'

Luke's face assumed a suitably mortified hue.

'So what's it to be?' pressed the gunfighter, maintaining his hard line.

'I didn't mean nothing, Snake,' he pleaded. 'And it won't happen again. Honest.'

Unseen by the kid, the gunfighter gave his sidekick a wry wink.

'Now we've gotten that sorted,' he said sternly, 'watch over the horses while we suss out the lie of the land.'

Without waiting for a reply, he hammered on the heavy door of the jailhouse with his pistol butt.

A muffled croak from within followed after the third attempt.

The two men pushed into the gloomy interior of the small office. Motes of dust floated in the static beams of light angling through a barred window. In a corner, a large black pot of coffee simmered atop a pot-bellied stove. Over to their left was a locked gunrack containing six repeating rifles.

Always of particular interest to ex-road agents entering a law office was the noticeboard on the back wall. A half-dozen penned sketches were depicted of various characters wanted for offences that included bank robbery, murder and extortion. It was no surprise that none of the mean-eyed hardcases on view was known to either of the visitors.

Times had moved on since their day on the owlhoot trail.

'What can I do for yuh?' grunted a large man who had only managed to lever himself out of a swing chair with some degree of effort.

A half-empty whiskey bottle on the scarred desk indicated where the jigger's attention had been focused prior to being disturbed. It was an unsmiling face that surveyed the newcomers, one that had not seen a razor in some time. This was clearly not a welcome visit.

'Sheriff's outa town and won't be back until the end of the week,' continued the surly lawdog. 'I'm the deputy in charge while he's away. Name of Ben Drukker.' A pudgy finger jabbed at a tin star on his brown leather vest hoping to emphasize his authority.

This news was music to Randy's ear. The chief lawman was away leaving this sorry specimen in charge. His blank expression gave nothing away.

'I hear tell you have a prisoner who needs legal representation,' he announced firmly in a cultivated accent imbued with a hint of arrogance. 'My name is Taylor Wagstaffe of Wagstaffe and Fortescue, attorneys-at-law. This is my partner, Mr Fortescue.' Shake Hands locked his face into a suitably haughty mode that he could barely contain. 'The reason for our somewhat dishevelled appearance' – Randy brushed a speck of dust from his shoulder – 'is due to our having been on the road for five days.'

From past experience, he knew that a high-blown accent always had the effect of chastening a bellicose lawman. He was counting on the fact that Concho Sterling had not already found a lawyer.

'C-Certainly, gentlemen,' fawned the contrite starpacker, quickly abandoning his previously suspicious attitude. 'If you would just surrender your weapons, I will take you through to the cell block.'

'Of course, Deputy,' said Randy, as they handed over their guns.

At the end of a narrow, dark passageway and around a corner were three cells. Only one was occupied. Another positive sign.

Drukker hung around after he'd informed the prisoner that his legal representatives had arrived.

'If we could have a few moments to discuss our client's case, it would be much appreciated,' warbled Randy, an obsequious smile pasted to his face. 'In private, if possible.'

Drukker nodded as he backed out, almost bowing in deference to the two tricksters. Once the heavy door had banged shut, Hands burst out laughing. He slapped his thigh in glee.

The prisoner was not so amused. Indeed, he was baffled at the outburst as the two bogus lawyers grinned at him through the bars. Immediately they had entered the cellblock, both men instantly recognized their old partner-in-crime. Heavier in build and greying around the temples, he was still the good-looking dude of yesteryear.

Randy shook his head feigning disapproval.

'Some guys just can't keep their pecker in check,' scoffed Hands, mockingly.

The bewildered prisoner looked from one to the other. Then Randy skewered him with the celebrated snaked-eyed regard.

That was when the penny dropped.

Concho's bright blue eyes gleamed. The firm jawline relaxed into a broad grin displaying a set of perfect teeth whiter than an Arctic fox. His delicately manicured hands eagerly reached through the bars grasping those of his old *compadres.*

For a long minute Concho was speechless, utterly dumbfounded.

Once the prisoner's voice had returned, he yammered, 'I just never would have recognized you fellas after all these years.'

'That's what ten years' hard labour does for you,' stated Randy. The comment emerged as a guttural rasp, although there was no guilt-loaded intention meant.

'Not to mention an acid-tongued wife,' Hands added with a sour grimace.

'We heard tell that some silver-sporting hick had

gotten hisself locked up for getting caught muscling in on the mayor's wife,' resumed the gunfighter.

'Had to be ol' Concho,' interposed Hands, wagging a reproachful finger.

'And we couldn't let our old buddy be the main guest at a neck-tie party without us getting involved, could we?' smiled Randy.

'So all we gotta do now is figure out a way of spiritin' you out of here.' This cogent observation from Shake Hands brought them all back down to earth.

'How much longer do you need, Mr Wagstaffe?'

The call echoing down the corridor from Deputy Drukker made them realize that time was not on their side.

'One minute and we'll be out,' replied Randy.

A few brief questions to their old buddy revealed that the trial was booked for the end of the week after the sheriff had returned. And it was to be held before His Honour, Judge Henry Jackson. A hanging judge to be sure!

'Seems like there was a bank robbery in Ouray,' Sterling explained regarding the sheriff's absence.

Hands laughed. 'Brings back old memories.'

'And he signed up all the best gun hands for the posse,' continued the prisoner.

Randy was more pragmatic. 'It also means the only law in Telluride is delivered by that turkey out yonder.'

The keys to the office door rattled meaningfully as the chafing deputy entered the cellblock.

'We'll come see you again tomorrow,' Randy

informed the prisoner retreating down the corridor. Then, for Drukker's benefit, 'And be assured, Mr Sterling, that with Wagstaffe and Fortescue as defence attorneys, you are in the very best of hands.'

Shake couldn't resist a brief chuckle.

Once out on the street, Luke was given the job of delivering their mounts to the livery stable for the night.

'And if'n the ostler charges you more'n two bits a horse, tell the greaseball to stick his broom where the sun don't shine,' Shake Hands hollered out after the boy's retreating back.

Luke turned, eyes crinkling in oblivious perplexity. It was the old desperado's sly grin that illuminated the boy's innocence.

'Don't you worry none,' he replied with chirpy confidence. 'I'll make durned sure we get the best deal.'

Once the boy had departed, Randy booked them into a rooming-house down a side street. The sign advertised beds with clean sheets, a soft mattress and full breakfast.

Both men realized that they would certainly need a good sleep if their plan to rescue Concho Sterling was to succeed.

A plan to that effect, however, had yet to be formulated.

TWELVE

BLAZE OF GLORY

Over an evening meal of beef stew and dumplings at the Miners' Hash House, it was decided that a diversion needed to be effected. Some means of luring Ben Drukker out of the jailhouse to the far end of Telluride. And it would have to be a dramatic event. A shock to the system. One to scare the living daylights out of the indolent reprobate.

Randy's devious mind had been mulling over a stunt he had pulled once before in Alamogordo down New Mexico way when one his men had gotten hisself arrested. It had worked like a dream then. There was no reason why the same ruse shouldn't be pulled in Telluride.

A fire!

Nothing was likely to strike terror into the hearts of Telluride's citizens more than the possible reduction of their wood-built settlement to a heap of ash. And while the blaze was being tackled, they could free Concho and disappear into the great beyond.

Once a course of action had been agreed upon, they retired for the night secure in the knowledge that their quest was nearing its end.

The following morning, Randy once again visited his 'client' to appraise him of their plan.

'What building have you in mind to fire up?' enquired Concho, his eyes bright with eager anticipation.

'Ain't given it much thought,' admitted the gunfighter stroking his stubbly chin. 'Just one at the east end of town as far from the hoosegow as possible. Once the whole caboodle has rushed up there, we come in here and bust you out. That's the plan anyhow.'

Concho mused on the notion. 'Didn't we pull that stunt in Alamogordo to free Chip Haynes?' Without waiting for a response, a gritty smirk creased the handsome features. 'Why not take out the mayor's house,' he suggested. 'The house will be empty. And I have it on good authority that Lily May, his widow, has gone to stay with her sister in Ouray.' A wistful expression bathed his classic profile. 'That Lily May sure is one classy dame. A pity that clunk of a husband returned when he did.'

'Especially for him,' commented a pensive Logan Hands.

Randy shook his head knowingly. 'You and that itchy pecker. When this is all over. I'm gonna have you gelded.'

'Just you try, mister,' laughed Concho, rubbing his

crotch suggestively.

'Well, at least if the place is empty,' Randy hurried on, bringing the conversation back onto a serious vein, 'then no one'll get hurt.'

'Yeh!' agreed Concho. 'And the powers-that-be will certainly want to save an important residence like that.'

A call from Ben Drukker brought the meeting to an end.

'Be ready at around midnight,' whispered Randy. 'That's when we set the cat among the pigeons.'

The rest of that day passed slowly. All three partners remained tense and expectant. They were aware of what the onset of darkness would bring, trusting to good judgement and a modicum of luck that all would go well.

Logan Hands bought two gallons of lamp oil just before the general store closed for the night. It was concealed behind the livery stable under some straw. Randy negotiated the purchase of a fresh horse for their new partner with the livery ostler.

A half-hour before the appointed time, Hands recovered the oil and made his way via a circuitous route along to the mayor's residence. It was a large two-storeyed structure constructed of white-painted clapboard. And most important of all, no lights were visible. He was thus able to douse the outer walls liberally with oil.

More so than the old hands, Luke was on edge the whole day. He had been given the job of running down the street spot on the hour of midnight and hollering out the dreaded warning of a conflagration at the mayor's house. Randy encouraged him to imbue his delivery with panic-stricken urgency.

That time had now arrived.

An owl hooted in the distance, an eerie sound that did nothing to calm his trembling frame.

As soon as he saw the initial glow of the flames at the edge of town, Luke sucked in a deep breath and emitted a high-pitched wail as he dashed headlong down the street. The spine-tingling ululation possessed all the discordant caterwauling of a wounded coyote.

'Fire! Fire!' he howled. 'The town's going up in flames. Get the fire tender out quick!'

Arriving at the sheriff's office, he hammered on the locked door.

'Deputy Drukker, get out here fast!'

The terrifying screech saw the door flung open in an instant.

'What in hell's name is all the fuss?' he railed, trying to shrug off the lethargic effects of the bourbon he had been copiously sampling.

'There's a fire broken out at the far end of town,' the boy shouted. 'You best come quick else it might spread.'

Drukker had been on the receiving end of a conflagration some years before when much of Tombstone had gone up in flames. It was a frightening prospect.

'You go inform the mayor, kid,' he rapped, already

hurrying up the street. 'I'll get a detail of bucket haulers together from the saloon.'

Any consideration that his prisoner had been left unguarded was forgotten.

Once the deputy was out of sight, Randy appeared from the alley adjoining the dressmaker's emporium where he had gleefully witnessed the successful accomplishment of their subterfuge.

'Well done, boy!' The praise brought a proud smile to Luke's pale complexion. 'Now get round to the back of the jailhouse and have the mounts ready for a quick getaway while I release Concho.'

'What about Shake?' asked the boy.

'Once he's sure the fire has a firm hold,' Randy informed the boy, 'he'll take that back trail we scouted earlier today and meet us a couple of miles west of town.

'Now, on your way,' he chivvied the boy. Once Luke had departed, he quickly entered the law office, six-shooter in hand.

The room was empty. On the desk top sat the bunch of cell keys, splayed out and just waiting to be commandeered. Unlocking the gun rack, Randy broke out a Winchester rifle. To one side was a black shellbelt with its holstered Smith & Wesson Schofield. After all these years, he instantly recognized the preferred sidearm of his old *compadre.*

The cellblock door was soon opened.

Pausing on the threshold, he cocked an ear to the swell of noise outside. As the flames took a firm hold, the entire population appeared to be gravitating towards the town's eastern limits. Blurry shadows flitted past the window. Nobody accorded the jailhouse more than a passing glance, all eyes being focused on the expanding conflagration. Already, hungry tongues of orange flame were grappling with the house adjoining that of the mayor.

Randy smiled. Logan Hands had done his job well.

Then he hustled long the cellblock passage, quickly opening up the barred door to release Concho Sterling.

That's when he heard a cry from the rear, instantly followed by the sharp crack of a pistol.

Behind the solid brick wall of the jail, Luke was nervously keeping the mounts in check. Whispering endearments into flaring nostrils, he threw a series of restive glances every which way. It was while he was eyeing the right-hand window high up on the wall where Sterling was in custody that a brittle challenge from behind broke the intensity of his concentration.

'What you a-doin' of round here?' demanded a gruff voice, edged with menacing defiance.

Luke was too stunned to reply.

'This looks mighty suspicious to me,' continued the threatening presence now emerging from the gloom. A hard-faced critter sporting a thick beard cautiously approached the boy. Cody Shanks had wandered down the alley to relieve himself before following the crowds. The puzzled frown twisting his weathered features intimated a degree of uncertainty as to what he had unexpectedly blundered upon.

Understanding could not be too far behind. 'You get down from there and come with me,' he rapped. 'We'll see what Ben Drukker has to say about this.'

Grabbing hold of the bridle of Luke's black stallion, Shanks reached for his holstered pistol. The threatening move stimulated the boy into retaliation.

'Take your hands off my horse.' Luke's reaction was surprisingly resolute and determined under the circumstances as he reached for his own weapon. Had the other jigger not been a touch the worse for drink, the outcome might have been different.

Without any hesitation, the boy hauled back the trigger of the .41 Lightning and fired. A thin spear of flame lanced from the short barrel. Cody Shanks staggered back clutching at his chest. His mouth opened in surprise. Then he pitched forward onto his face.

Luke just sat there, immobile, incapable of movement. Wisps of smoke twined from the small gun still clutched in his right hand. This was the second man he had killed. How many more would follow? The thought despatched a chilled ripple down his spine.

It was Randy Cole who jerked his mind back to the reality of their situation.

'Leather that gun, kid, and let's get moving,' he snapped roughly, shaking the boy's trembling shoulder. Luke Bowdry may be his kin but this was no time for tenderhearted ministrations. They needed to disappear into the night before that shot attracted any more unwelcome attention. The nature of what had taken place in the alley could be analysed once the dust had settled.

He slapped the black's rump firmly. The big horse jumped forward forcing Luke to take control as he followed Randy and the newly released Concho Sterling across a series of back lots in a general westerly direction. The glow from the burning buildings to the east was mounting in intensity.

Slowly the crackle of blistering timbers and shattered glass faded into the opacity of night as they headed west.

Rampant infernos had a voracious appetite devouring all in their path. Randy hoped that the Telluride populace had Lady Luck on their side. He derived no pleasure from being witness to a town's destruction.

Once they were well clear of the danger zone, a temporary halt was called as he cast an unsettled gaze over their backtrail. There was no sign of any pursuit. Everybody appeared to be focused on tackling the fire.

Sterling read his thoughts, a measure of guilt weighing upon his usually blithe demeanour.

'Them guys'll have it under control in no time,' he averred. 'I seen 'em practising only two days ago.'

'Main thing is we sprung you,' added Hands jumping to his defence. The ex-storekeeper had reached the meeting place before them.

Sterling arrowed a quizzical look towards his old boss. 'Any chance of you letting me in on the real reason for this breakout?'

Randy reciprocated the puzzled concern with one

that implied wily machinations in abundance.

'All in good time, Concho.' The arcane smile hinted of no regrets regarding the rescue of his confederate. 'All in good time.'

The latest member of the gang sighed.

Same old Randy, he mused. All would be revealed when the time was right, and not before. It had been the same when a new bank job was being planned all those years ago. Nonetheless, he was more than a little intrigued as to what the snaked-eyed gunfighter had in mind this time around.

Only when the false dawn announced its presence in the form of yellow and purple streaks slicing across the eastern sky did Randy call a halt. They had cut across country taking a course due west over the San Miguel Flats. The undulating terrain was easier on the horses enabling them to maintain a steady canter throughout the night.

Over a breakfast of refried beans, tortillas and coffee, Randy filled his latest recruit in on what had to be done. He had taken it for granted that the carefree lady's man would be willing to go along with whatever scheme was devised for rescuing Jan Bowdry.

He was not disappointed. And learning that Jute Farley had instigated the abduction after killing his old partner, Clint, only served to intensify the younger man's resolve.

Concho did, however, have one reservation.

'What about the kid?' he enquired, once Luke had been sent down to the river-bank to water the horses.

'This ain't gonna be no Sunday afternoon picnic.'

'I felt the same way,' concurred Randy. 'But he knows the score, not to mention his way around firearms. And he's a stubborn young dude just like his father.' A paternal smile settled on the boy's distant form. 'Twice now he's gotten me out of tough scrapes.'

No mention was made of Randy's true relationship with the boy. And Concho accepted his old leader's evaluation without argument. Removing a thin cigar from his vest pocket, he lit up, relishing the taste.

'So what's the plan?'

Randy's thick eyebrows lifted.

That was the thousand-dollar question, the key issue still to be determined.

And there was no way it could effectively be thrashed out until they were all in a position to survey the lie of the land at Bullfrog Basin.

THIRTEEN

BULLFROG BLITZ

Jan Bowdry had managed to get a full night's sleep. It was her first such luxury since that terrible day when Jute Farley had arrived and carried her off from the homestead. No amount of pleading for more time had swayed the brutal outlaw's warped mind. He was determined to have his way, and Jan had been forced to stomach his carnal desires on a regular basis ever since.

Thankfully, he had left her alone the previous night. It was a brief respite for which she gave thanks to whatever God was still keeping her in the land of the living. How long she had been stuck in this bestial encampment was impossible to calculate. Days and nights had merged into a hellish purgatory that seemed endless.

But hope springs eternal in the human breast. Concealed deep within her soul was the fervent aspiration that Luke had managed somehow to find the one man who could bring an end to this torment.

The four riders had reached the south rim of Bullfrog Basin the previous evening and had made camp in a small cave. They were lying prone overlooking the expansive encampment that Jute Farley had appropriated. On the far side, the stark precipice of streaked sandstone radiated a refulgent orange in the early light of a new dawn.

Although he could not see a guard, Randy made certain that none of his *compadres* exposed themselves. His last encounter with Buffalo Jacks was still fresh in his mind notwithstanding the fact that Squint Regan had assured him that no sentries were ever posted on this side of the basin.

The outlaw had also willingly proffered the vital knowledge that a concealed crack in the mesa wall allowed access to the camp from the rear. Something the outlaw had discovered by accident only a week previously while out hunting.

That essential link was to be their means of entry and exit, hopefully without announcing their presence before Jan Bowdry had been rescued.

Scanning the camp, even at this early hour a hive of activity, Randy's major preoccupation was to discover where Farley was holding the captive. Numerous female camp followers were wandering about preparing the first meal of the day. Some had children in tow. But none of the women bore any resemblance to Jan.

It was a dry and desolate place. Crazy dust devils

sprinted across the sandy flats egged on by a stiff breeze, their headlong dash abruptly terminated by the numerous clumps of mesquite.

Randy scratched his head. Tight lines ribbed his brow, a poignant testimony to the burgeoning level of frustration.

'How in the name of a lop-eared mule are we gonna find out where that Judas is keeping her?' The terse query displayed an obvious sense of exasperation. 'There ain't no point us going in there blind. Farley would have the whip hand.'

'Seems like the varmint is still holding all the aces,' agreed a reluctant Shake Hands.

'I could go down,' piped up a reedy voice.

The others turned as one to peer at Luke Bowdry.

'Makes a heap of sense,' he hurried on eagerly. 'None of them skunks would notice another young kid in their midst. I could scout around and find the hut where Ma's being held then give you a signal when I've found her.'

No word was uttered. Although Luke's suggestion was the perfect answer to their dilemma, it had to be Randy's decision. He was torn between rescuing his one true love, and exposing his new-found son to such a perilous endeavour. Stuck between a rock and a hard place, Randy Cole dithered.

Luke pressed home his point.

'This is the only way forward,' he urged. 'And it's not as if them turkeys are gonna plug a young squirt like me.' His comment was followed by a hollow laugh, but it was devoid of any humour.

A long minute passed during which time the snake-eyed boss struggled desperately with his conscience to come up with the correct course of action. The tight jawline betrayed his quandary. Eventually he shifted a resolute gaze towards Luke.

Grasping the boy's shoulders with both hands, he firmly, yet with a deep conviction, impressed on the boy of the need to stay out of trouble. To avoid any unnecessary risks. A futile consideration, but it had to be voiced.

Luke nodded before lowering himself into the narrow fissure that terminated behind a cluster of desiccated cottonwoods a half-mile up valley from the main camp. It was some time later that Randy picked out the boy casually strolling into view.

He had somehow got hold of a bucket giving the impression that he had been to fetch water from the creek. Clever kid, thought Randy, smiling to himself.

A dull light filtered through the thin rag covering the adobe room's only window. It occurred to Jan's torpid mind that something alien to her surroundings had woken her up.

She sucked in a deep breath. There was some other presence in the spartan room. Please, not Jute Farley! Surely the brute could allow her one night of peace. A constrained gasp escaped from gritted teeth as she raised herself onto one elbow.

'Who's there?' she croaked. The fretful voice was hoarse and full of trepidation.

A shadow flitted across the earth floor.

'Easy, Ma,' came back the equally emotive response. 'It's only me.'

'Luke?' Jan eyes bulged. Her angelic features were pinched into a disbelieving rictus. 'Is that you?' She squeezed her eyes tight shut, not wanting the mirage to dissolve into a nightmare. Slowly opening one eye, she ascertained that the figure was still there. Grabbing hold of the boy, she hugged him close to her bosom. 'B-But what are you doing here?'

Eventually the boy levered himself free of her fearful embrace. He knew that any minute, one of the gang could appear and expose the charade.

'I found Randy Cole,' he said.

'Randy's here?' Jan could scarcely credit that her incarceration might be over. 'But where is he?' It was clear that her son was alone.

'I've sneaked in here to locate where Farley has you holed up. The guys are up on the south rim waiting on my signal. There's only four of us. Two of Randy's old sidekicks, and me.'

Jan shook her head. A fresh wave of panicky thoughts jostled for supremacy in her fevered brain.

'But three men and a boy won't stand a chance aganst Farley. He has at least a dozen hard-bitten gunhands to back him up,' she exclaimed. Then her voice hardened. 'And I won't have my son involved in any gunplay.'

'Too late for all that, Ma,' the boy asserted firmly. 'I'm a full member of the Cole Gang now.'

'But, Luke—'

'I ain't got time for no arguments, Ma,' interjected

the boy. 'My job was to find out where you were being held. I've done that now. And don't forget that we've got the element of surprise on our side,' he added, trying to reassure the distraught woman. After kissing his mother tenderly on the cheek, Luke sidled quietly towards the door. 'I have to go now. Randy's waitin' on my signal. And don't you fret none: his sole aim is to get you safely out of here. Evening the score with Farley can come later.'

And with that he was gone.

Jan squeezed her eyes tight shut. She was hard pressed to deny that Luke's unexpected appearance had all been a mesmeric fantasy. A hateful trick of the mind, Any minute now she would awake to the awful reality of her situation, the brutal lusting face of Jute Farley grinning down at her.

'There's the signal.'

Concho Sterling aimed a gloved finger towards a group of adobe dwellings lying in the shelter of a huge overhang on the far side of the basin. He raised his own arm in acknowledgement then quickly withdrew it.

'OK, boys,' hissed Randy. 'Let's go!'

It had been decided that Luke would meet them at the base of the ravine and inform them where his mother was being confined. They would then have to figure out the best means of spiriting her away.

Careful to avoid dislodging any loose stones, the three men edged their way tentatively down the fissure. It was a rough, steeply shelving gully that threaded a snake-like course down between layers of fractured rock. The descent took longer than expected but was eventually completed without mishap.

At the base of the hidden cleft, they ducked down behind some boulders to await Luke's arrival. All three had palmed their revolvers. The tension was almost palpable in the hot fetid air of the enclosed basin. When viewed from below, the exit of their escape route was invisible at valley level due to the entrance being shrouded by a thick cloak of trees.

Luke suddenly appeared from behind a square building.

'What's the word, boy?' snapped Randy, unable to swallow the brittleness in his voice. 'You found where Jan's being held?'

Luke nodded. He indicated a squat structure separated from the others on the far side of the clearing.

'And the door wasn't even locked,' he panted, trying to suck oxygen into his straining lungs.

'In a camp like this, there ain't no need for locks,' observed Hands philosophically. 'The skunk knows the only way out is through the gorge which is well guarded.'

'But we know different, eh, guys?' smiled Concho, slinging a thumb behind to the constricted ravine down which they had so recently shimmied.

Randy's practised eye quickly absorbed the intervening terrain. To reach the hut, they would need to circle around to the left making effectual use of the limited cover available. Luck was assuredly going to play a vital role in their rescue mission.

'I also spotted Farley,' declared Luke.

Randy's head snapped up. His fists clenched tight, thin lips drawn back in a hard line of hate. So the bastard was here.

But their first priority was to rescue Jan. Farley could be dealt with once that had been accomplished successfully.

'Keep your eyes peeled,' he ordered, leading the way across the open ground, ducking low to reduce any chance of being detected. With the early morning sun barely above the eastern horizon, most of the Farley gang had not yet surfaced. A boon that Randy had been counting upon.

They reached the collection of adobe hutments without the alarm having been raised. Randy directed Concho to keep watch behind a crumbling wall that faced the door of the squat room where Jan Bowdry was secreted. Hands instinctively slipped across to the side wall of the dwelling where he could cover the exit.

Randy instructed Luke to go back to the ravine and keep watch. In truth he wanted the boy out of the way just in case lead started to fly.

Once the boy had departed at the run, a final scan of the basin revealed only a handful of women whose attention was fully absorbed with preparing breakfast. Randy checked his revolver then scuttled along the front edge of the mud brick hut and quickly disappeared inside.

He had been inside the room no more than a

minute when gunfire erupted from the direction of the hidden ravine.

Luke had been so intent on looking back to where his mother was being held that he failed to notice a man who had just emerged from another building close by. Spider Webb had been making an early check on the gang's stock of dynamite. The boss had intimated they were going to start blasting in the next few days. He hadn't deigned to explain, and Webb hadn't asked.

The burly tough had just emerged from the hut when Luke ran slap bang into him. Both were taken completely by surprise and tumbled into the dust. But it was the outlaw who recovered first.

'Who the hell are you?' demanded Webb, grabbing hold of the boy's arm. 'I ain't seen you before.' He twisted Luke's arm up his back, the other encircling the boy's neck. Luke yelped in pain. Webb's beady eyes glinted in triumph. A growl of anger escaped from behind the straggly beard. 'You're comin' with me, kid. The boss will want to know what your game is.'

But Luke Bowdry was not prepared to submit without a fight. A chance to turn the tables was offered as the outlaw's grip relaxed. It was now or never. He jabbed his right boot heel down onto the outlaw's foot.

This time it was Spider Webb who yelled aloud as he leapt in the air grabbing at his injured appendage.

Taking advantage of the sudden change in

fortunes, Luke snatched the Colt Lightning from its holster. Without any hesitation he fired two slugs into the stricken outlaw.

Webb's body jerked as the lethal hunks of lead slammed into his barrel chest at point-blank range. He reeled drunkenly under the impact, sank to his knees and keeled over.

The spider had been well and truly caught in his own webb.

Luke's arms fell to his side. Shock once again registered on his stunned face threatening to immobilize him.

But the strident echo of the gunshots had not gone unnoticed. Already men were emerging from numerous huts, guns to hand and wondering what all the commotion was about.

Jute Farley was one of the first. His initial reaction was that some early bird was out hunting. He cursed the varmint aloud for having disturbed his time with one of the camp girls. The culprit was gonna pay dearly for this. Any thought that the camp had been infiltrated never occurred to him.

'Hey, Ches!' he called to one of his men. 'Who in tarnation is causin' all that ruckus?'

Chester Bannock shrugged. Then he pointed towards the hut over on the far side of the basin from which Randy Cole had just materialized.

'Over there, boss!' he hollered.

Farley only had time to register the fact that his prisoner was being rescued when more gunfire erupted from behind a wall. A bullet whistled past his left ear prompting an immediate retreat behind the side of a nearby hut. Drawing his own pistol, he snapped a couple of shots back in reply.

It had all happened in the blink of an eye. None the less, Farley had recognized the interloper. That shock of straw hair and the livid cheek scar gleaming white in the early morning sun meant only one thing.

Snake-eyed Randy Cole!

By some quirk of fate, his old confederate had somehow tracked him down.

Ripples of fear traced a path along the outlaw's back. Beads of sweat bubbled up on his forehead. Buried deep within the recesses of his warped mind for all this time, the Judas's betrayal once again reared its ugly head.

But Jute Farley was not so easily panicked.

He peered round the corner of the mud hut noting that Cole and the woman were heading towards the top end of the valley. A twisted smirk broke across the swarthy features. It was a dead end with no way out. They were trapped.

All the same he could not afford to be complacent. As if to remind him that danger was still lurking close by, chunks of hard mud burst from the wall inches above his head accompanied by the sharp report of pistol fire. He ducked back. This was no place to mount a counter attack.

He shouted to his men who were running around like headless chickens desperately seeking cover of their own. The surprise attack had taken the entire camp unawares.

'Cover me while I get inside,' he rasped. He pointed to the low palisade behind which Logan Hands was sheltering.

A fusillade of hot lead drove the attacker down giving Farley the opportunity to slip round the side of the building and back inside through the open door. Pushing aside the Indian girl with whom he had spent the night, the outlaw chieftain scuttled up a ladder and through a square aperture onto the flat roof

Gingerly he slithered across to the low parapet and peered over. Hands was clearly in view. But his attention was fully absorbed by the fearsome volley emanating from Farley's men. Jacking a round into his Winchester, he took careful aim gently squeezing the hair trigger. The rosewood butt slammed into his shoulder. An instant later, Farley had the satisfaction of witnessing the exposed pate exploding in a gory mess of blood and brain matter.

One down, but how many to go?

The expected response to Hands's grisly demise came from the corner of the women's living quarters.

Another bolt from the blue now revealed itself. Silver discs in the hat band could belong to only one person – Concho Sterling. It appeared that Jute Farley's nemesis had gathered the old gang together. And they were obviously intent on avenging Clint Bowdry and rescuing his wife.

Not if he had anything to do with it.

Farley surveyed his dithering forces.

'Move yourselves,' he harangued them vehemently. 'Don't let the critters escape. The man who brings me the woman unharmed will get a thousand bucks extra in his wage packet.'

Concho emptied his pistol at the advancing hoard of dollar-hungry hard-asses. He had the satisfaction of seeing two of them go down. Then his pistol clicked onto an empty chamber. Scrambling crab-like towards the low wall over which the body of Logan Hands was draped, he snatched up his amigo's abandoned rifle. Lead shot buzzed around him like a swarm of angry hornets.

Randy paused, indicating for Jan to stay low. He despatched two shots towards the steadily advancing outlaws. A thousand-dollar bonus was a hefty incentive but not if you didn't live to spend it. The initial rush faltered.

'Shift yer damned asses,' howled Farley from the rear. 'I ain't payin' you red-necks to sit around all day. There's only two of 'em.'

'Take the woman and go!' urged Concho jabbing his arm towards the hidden ravine. 'I'll keep these varmints pinned down and join you later.'

Randy nodded his thanks. He hated leaving his *compadre* but rescuing Jan had to be given prority.

'Don't be too long,' he exhorted the younger man. 'We have to get even with Farley, remember.'

Concho responded with a thumbs up then turned, letting his rifle do all the talking.

FOURTEEN

BETRAYAL AVENGED

The two fugitives hurried away. They reached the base of the ravine fifteen minutes later where Luke was anxiously waiting. His mother hugged her son with a passionate fervour.

Then she looked across to her saviour. There was a strange slant in her brown eyes that Randy was hard pressed to construe. Was it for him or the boy? No comment had passed between them since the rescue.

Then she spoke.

'I knew you'd come.' The words emerged as a soft burr but contained the firm conviction that held more than mere gratitude. For Randy Cole it was enough. He knew that the journey back from the shattered remnants of his past had been worthwhile.

It was Luke who broke the spell.

'Where are the others?' he asked.

As Randy narrowed his gaze back towards the warring encampment, a whoop of triumph rang out. A macabre silence ensued, hauntingly intense and equally dreadful in its magnitude. Randy's face assumed an ashen hue. Concho was down. And the rats were hot on their tail.

'There ain't no time to lose,' he cried, leading the way through the dense thicket to the base of the rift. 'Take your ma up the trail, while I try to hold 'em off,' he entrusted Luke.

The boy hesitated.

'Hurry it up, kid,' snapped the gunfighter. 'We ain't got time for parleying.'

That was when Luke removed a couple of white tubes from inside his jacket. They looked remarkably like sticks of dynamite.

'Is that what I think it is?' beamed Randy, a sudden elation lifting his sombre mood.

'Took them off some dude who I kinda bumped into,' preened the boy nonchalantly. 'I persuaded him that strumming a harp would be a more fitting occupation.'

Randy shot him a louring grimace. If they came out of this in one piece, the boy was going to need re-educating. Until then. . . .

The growing tumult of an approaching confrontation nudged Randy back to the present and the grim situation which had to be neutralized. But good fortune was shining down on them. The sticks were already primed with a twenty-second fuse.

He urged mother and son to begin the arduous

climb while he quickly yet expertly planted the explosives to secure the maximum effect. One positioned on either side of the narrow fissure would effectively block any possibility of continued pursuit. And if he set them to go off at the right moment, maybe it would take out the bulk of their pursuers.

Timing was all important.

Only when he could hear them blundering through the tree cover did he strike a vesta and apply it to the fuse. With so short a time span, he quickly turned and followed the others up the steeply canting track. Loose stones scattering away beneath his boots lent urgency to the upward climb.

It seemed like a lifetime before the dull crump of high explosive informed Randy that his plan had succeeded. The roar of dislocating rock hammered at his eardrums. Smoke billowing up the constricted flue was accompanied by a searing blast of hot air.

Randy flattened himself against the rough ground, the shattering reverberation plucking at his clothing. Debris rained down onto his exposed body, but thankfully nothing too large. The grumble of shifting rock continued for some time as loose and dislodged flakes broke away from the bedrock.

The sound of pursuit died with the blocking of the secret ravine.

Then another sound assailed his ears. It was faint but unmistakable, emanating from the heights above.

'Are you all right, Randy? Please let me know!'

The desperate cry for reassurance was clearly

evident in Jan Bowdry's plaintive supplication.

Then another plea came. One that brought a lump to his throat, and more than a tear to his eye.

'Pa! Pa! Please let us know you're still alive.'

So. Jan had told the boy the truth. He bowed his dust-caked head and gave thanks to his Maker.

'I'll be with you in the shake of raccoon's tail,' he assured them both. The crack in his voice betrayed the depth of feeling that Luke's revelation had engendered in the ageing gunfighter.

The reunion on the crest of the mesa was nothing if not emotional. They hugged each other then and cried bucketfuls of tears. Although Jan had suffered badly at the hands of the her odious abductor, she still managed to retain the dignity and poise for which the gunfighter had always held her in the highest esteem. Nor had she lost that elegant beauty he remembered so well.

Almond eyes of deepest mahogany held him fast in their hypnotic trance.

Many years had passed them both by, many thoughts left unsaid. Yet after all this time, they both felt tongue-tied, unsure of mouthing the right words. But this was not the moment for reminiscing.

Randy's pragmatic character reminded him that his task was not yet complete. There remained the problem of dealing with Jute Farley. By now the skulking Judas would have known that his days on the Dirty Devil were numbered.

Where would the double-dealing polecat head for now?

Another quandary the gunfighter needed to straighten out was the reasoning behind the eviction of homesteaders from the valley. That answer could only be found in Monticello and the office of the Green River Development Agency. Randy surmised that his adversary would make for there initially to get paid off. No doubt he would omit to inform the agent of the details regarding the failure of his mission.

'Is there some place you could stay while I go after Jute Farley?' Randy enquired of the comely female. Already he was reloading his revolver and checking the action of his rifle.

Jan could read into what he was thinking.

'Forget about that toad,' she urged him biting her lower lip. 'He's finished around here now. We'll inform the sheriff at Monticello. Let him take care of things.' It was a half-hearted attempt to make Randy walk a safer line. Yet in her heart, she knew that such a plea would fall upon stony ground.

She was not wrong in that assumption.

A cold, hard look now replaced the warmth of moments before.

'You know I have to see this through,' he uttered, in a flat monotone.

'Even if he guns you down?' she stressed, clutching his arm tightly. 'Farley's a scheming dog who don't play by the rules.'

A harsh laugh issued from between clenched teeth.

'Neither do I, Jan, neither do I!'

'Take me with you, Randy,' prompted Luke, stepping forward and ignoring his mother's plea to the contrary. 'We make a great team, don't we?'

'We sure do, son,' smiled the gunfighter ruffling the boy's touseled hair. 'But I need you to take care of your ma. You do that for me and I promise we'll make up for lost time when I return. What d'yuh say, partner?'

'Well, if you say so, Pa.'

Randy turned away to hide the emotion bubbling up inside. Mounting up, he rode away without looking back, a single arm raised in salute.

Randy drew rein on the edge of Monticello. Carefully, he surveyed the busy main street, snake-eyes probing the dusty air for anything unusual. Anything that might initially offer him a clue as to whether Jute Farley was still in town. He would have had a good hour's start. And the trail from Bullfrog Basin was much easier than that which the gunfighter had been forced to negotiate down from the boulder-strewn heights of the mesa country.

Nothing appeared untoward so he squeezed the sorrel with his knees, gently nudging the horse forward. At the same time he flicked off the hammer thong securing the .45 in its holster.

The regular jabber of a town in full flow was abruptly split by a strident gnashing of teeth. Randy tensed. But it was merely a scruffy mutt bounding from an alley in pursuit of a squealing cat. A line of black crows on a rooftop squawked in unison. A warning maybe for the gunfighter to watch his step?

Halfway down the street, he stopped in front of the agency office. It seemed like many moons had passed since he'd last called here to see Jethro Tindale. The guy had a heap of explaining to do.

Entering the lobby, he walked straight over to the manager's office. A lackey tried to block his path but was unceremoniously brushed aside.

'You can't go in there without an appointment,' he howled scrambling to his feet and dusting down his tight suit. 'Mister Tindale is busy.'

'Well if it ain't the ever helpful Ephraim Stokes,' grinned Randy suggestively tapping the butt of his revolver. 'So we meet again.'

Stokes gulped as recognition showed on his ashen face.

'Now get out of my way if'n you don't want a visit from the undertaker.' The revolver jumped into the palm of his hand encouraging the bumbling clerk to step quickly aside.

Randy shouldered through into the inner sanctum. But the room was empty.

'Hey, Ephraim!' shouted Randy to the retreating clerk's back. 'Didn't you just say the manager was busy?'

The man replied with a puzzled nod.

'Well, he ain't here now.'

The clerk spluttered as he entered the office. A petrified howl gushed from his gaping mouth. Then, trembling with fear, he pointed to a foot sticking out from behind the large oak desk.

Randy hustled round to get a closer look.

'Is it Mister. . . .'

'Sure is,' confirmed Randy with a sigh, 'And there ain't no chance of the jigger spilling the beans now.' A large bowie knife protruded from the dead agent's back.

'Did you let the killer in?' snapped Randy.

'N-no,' stuttered the clerk, dragging a handkerchief across his sweating brow. 'Mister Tindale said he did not want to be disturbed. I assumed he had important paperwork to complete.'

'Hm,' muttered Randy to himself. 'So you didn't see nobody come in?'

'Most definitely not.' The shaking clerk was emphatic on that point, hand over his mouth as he tried to control the contents of his stomach. This was the first time Ephraim Stokes had seen a dead body.

'Then he must have come in by the back door,' said Randy thinking aloud. 'When did you last see Tindale?'

The clerk blinked at the ticking clock on the wall. 'Must be about an hour since,' he said.

That was when Randy noticed the door to the large safe swinging open. He peered inside. A grim smile creased his taut features. 'And it looks as if the varmint helped himself to a hefty bonus while he was here.'

'You know who perpetrated this vile deed?' enquired the stunned clerk.

'Too right I do. And he can't have gone far if what you say is true.'

'I will go and inform the sheriff,' announced

Stokes, turning gratefully away from the grisly scene.

'No!' snapped Randy adamantly. 'I'll do that . . . once I've killed the treacherous rat.'

Gun in hand. Randy scooted back onto the main street.

'Where would the skunk go now?' he muttered to himself.

That was when he caught sight of the well-lathered cayuse. It was standing with its head bowed in front of the Brass Neck Saloon a block down on the far side. Traces of blood dripping from the animal's flanks indicated it had been ridden hard, and recently.

Randy bit his lip, then sucked in a deep breath of fresh air.

Jute Farley had to be inside.

Should he go in now? Or wait for the bastard to emerge and challenge him on the street?

The dilemma was solved as Jute Farley shouldered through the batwings onto the boardwalk. He was alone, a heavy saddle-bag slung over his left shoulder. Belching loudly, he hawked a lump of phlegm into the dust. A grim smile greased his ugly face.

Randy's face purpled in fury. Teeth grinding, his grip tightened on the revolver.

Farley clearly thought he had outwitted his adversary and had sufficient time on his hands to enjoy a few drinks before losing himself in the Utah badlands.

And so he would have had Randy not taken the short cut through the mountains by way of the

Rainbow Wedge. Luke had told him about the narrow gap that he had inadvertently come across one day the previous fall while on a hunting trip with his stepfather.

The moment of confrontation had arrived.

After all these years, the odious features of the traitor once again seared themselves onto his vision. As if in slow motion, he stepped down onto the dusty hardpack and moved towards his destiny. From far away the burbling cacophany appeared to dwindle. Curious bystanders watched as the vengeful stranger advanced down the middle of the street ignoring wagons and horses in his path as if they did not exist.

'What's goin' on?' came a demand from the rear.

'Looks like a gunfight,' observed a gruff voice in reply.

'Ain't had some'n like that since '78 when wild Bob Thornton took out Dutch Henry,' commented another.

When no more than twenty yards from the unsuspecting outlaw, Randy stopped and replaced the revolver in its holster. Flexing gloved hands in readiness for the retribution he had long harboured, Randy Cole focused his mind on what had to be done.

He felt neither hatred nor euphoria. Only a grim determination to avenge a wrong.

'Farley!'

The single word rang out. A resounding echo that bounced off the close-packed assembly.

Jute Farley froze. His jaw dropped. He would

recognize that voice anywhere. How in tarnation had the crafty galoot managed to get here so quick? Too late to fathom that one out now.

'Fill your hand and make your play,' came the blunt challenge. 'This is the end of the road, Jute. And it's been a long journey.'

Monticello held its breath. It seemed like the whole town had come out to witness the unusual phenomenon of a real one-on-one gunfight in their midst. Most killings in the town occurred under wraps with no witnesses. This showdown was in the open, a contest to the death.

Farley stepped down into the rutted street and sidled out to face his nemesis.

Silence reigned. Not a word issued from the assembled throng.

Even the sheriff who had been summoned by Ephraim Stokes maintained a discreet distance. Having been raised in the orthodox school of western chivalry, he understood that this was an age-old means by which antagonists righted their wrongs.

Both men assumed their stance, waiting, watching, muscles taut, nerves strung tighter than a banker's fist.

It all happened in a split second. The crash of gunfire. Smoke filling the air as death stretched out its icy hand.

The participants moved in synchronization. None of those watching could have sworn who had drawn their pistol first. Randy's hat flew skyward, his straw locks parted in the middle. He felt a seering pain from the hot bullet. The shock made him lurch back a pace. His own weapon had bucked three times to Farley's single shot.

The outlaw opened his mouth in obvious surprise. He had always reckoned himself faster. He was wrong. A splash of bright red stained his grey shirt where three slugs had smashed into him. His body folded at the knee.

Randy hurried across.

With Tindale dead, Farley was the only one left who could reveal the true reason for all the trouble on the Dirty Devil.

He grabbed the outlaw as he keeled over.

'Why did the agency want that land?' he demanded, desperately trying to shake some life back into the rapidly fading body. 'Spill it, damn you!'

Farley coughed. Gurgling blood spewed from his twisted mouth.

'Now wouldn't you . . . like to . . . know.'

An ugly scowl remained on the brutalized face as the outlaw breathed his last, the hard glassy stare laughing at his killer. It was as if Jute Farley had come out on top.

Randy threw the bloody corpse aside. Stumping back up the street, he mounted the sorrel and swung round retracing his steps. He had arranged to meet Jan Bowdry and her son at the ruins of their farm. From there they would work out what the future held for them all.

*

Mother and son were waiting when he crested the brow above the blackened hulk. Jan hurried across the yard to meet him.

'Don't ever leave me again, Randy Cole,' she fussed urgently, clasping the old gunfighter to her chest. 'We can always rebuild this place. And Luke needs a father. A real father this time.'

The boy arrived at a run to join in the celebration.

'I might be your blood kin, boy,' said the ex-bank robber, 'but don't ever suppose that I can replace Clint. He brought you up and raised you as his own. I can only hope to live up to those high standards.'

It was some time later when Jan had built a fire and was preparing a meal of rabbit stew with green beans that Luke produced a hunk of rock from inside his jacket. It gleamed yellow in the flickering embers of the fire.

'What's that you got there, Luke?' asked a curious Randy Cole.

'I was digging around over yonder.' Luke pointed to a low bluff lying in shadow on the far side of the ruins. He shrugged. 'Just something to keep my mind off . . . you know. Found it at the bottom of the crags.'

Leaning over, Randy took hold of the small chunk of rough stone and held it up to the light. His eyes bulged in shock.

Was this what he thought it was?